BEYOND
An Anthology

Edited by
Udith Dematagoda,
Stewart McCarthy and
Richard Porteous

HYPERIDEAN PRESS

Edinburgh

Hyperidean Press
Pilrig Street
Edinburgh
www.hyperideanpress.com

Publisher's Note: These are works of fiction. Names, characters, places, and incidents are products of each individual authors' imagination, and any resemblance to actual people, living or dead, or to businesses, companies, events, institutions, or locales is purely coincidental.

Design and Art Direction by Jamie Sunderland

Cover Artwork: 'Chromotography#5' by Sarah Bildstein, Copyright 2018

Beyond: An Anthology/ -- 1st edition, June 2020.
ISBN 978-1-9163767-2-4

Il faut être absolument moderne

—Arthur Rimbaud

CONTENTS

FOREWORD

This anthology was conceived in December 2019, on the precipice of a new decade. We wanted to reimagine and recover the idea of the future. Borne from an almost apocalyptic optimism, we desired to recapture all that was once exhilarating, bewildering and unsettling about such thinking, whilst rejecting the simplistic assumptions of a neoliberal consensus that propagates the limited novelty of 'innovation' as progress. In our open Call for Submissions, we asked for work that proceeded from the disconcerting notion that our current paradigm is one of chaos and disorder. We sought work that addressed the themes of polarization, disaffection, alienation, sensory over-stimulation, the destabilization of perception, the fraught and contented field of desire and other symptoms of emergent and quotidian psychopathologies. The works presented in this volume, in their own way, reflect these original aims.

We could not have predicted this current Global Pandemic, which in such a short space of time has torn apart our collective complacency and resignation towards what was previously thought immutable and monolithic. However, the cultural and aesthetic responses to this crisis have been entirely predictable. Instead of attempting to re-think what universalism means in the midst of a universal crisis for humanity, the cultural establishment has instead redoubled its efforts to champion the narrow subjectivity of identitarianism, atomisation and the various modes of narcissism masquerading as profundity. It's almost as though the aesthetic level of discourse has become completely interchangeable with that of ideology.

There is an unmistakable infantilism inculcated by contemporary culture, evident in every facet of cultural life, and no doubt exasperated by a pervasive atmosphere of technological alienation. A literary culture which relies too heavily on recycling, regurgitation and pandering is as worthless as one which finds solace in nostalgia and pastiche. The varied works presented here (enchanted, speculative, dystopian, weird) cannot be said to be uniform in their themes, form or content. Yet they all express a collective anxiety at the insufficiency of available conventions, generic or otherwise, to adequately address a world which seems to grow darker and more incomprehensible, even as its technologies grow more sophisticated and seamless.

We began Hyperidean Press to discover and promote new writing that recaptures something of the febrile vitality of those early twentieth century avant-gardes, which derived from an atmosphere of uncertainty and unrest not dissimilar to our own. But to do so, we must be absolutely modern - eschewing any hope of a return to some prelapsarian and mythical past. Original work which reflects the impulse to explore the variegated experiences of our modern life, from the abject to the sublime, still exists. Hopefully this modest anthology of stories will convince you of the same.

The Editors, May 2020

WOLF

Joe Alexander

CHILD

My father's gone. My mother's dead. I have no name. I am a monster, seed of devils and possessed by wraiths. People watch me. They wish to make me better, to drive out the wickedness and save my soul. My world is this room. And that room. This is my earth. Fifteen steps there, twenty-six there. As I grow, it shrinks. I'm a risk, a corruptor, a sour spirit. They tell me this and more. My father is a demon, nameless and ungodly. My mother was weak and disreputable and died as I burst from her womb. They tell me this.

They found me as a dog, small, vicious, living on four legs, eating rats. I snarled and roared and bit and scratched as they saved me. I stank of blood and shit and evil.

They saved me. They civilised me. They brought me here. They saved me because I am chosen and I will make change and be important. They tell me this. They brought me into their church, but my devils are deeper rooted than even they've seen. Before I have memories, this has been my world. This room and that room.

My first memory is pain. And screaming. And more pain, and more screaming until I stopped screaming and there was no new pain. Just old pain. And new scars.

They have few scars. Or none. I have many. They gave them to me. Some are gifts – to defend against darkness. Others are punishments, for I am slow and infinitely bad.

I was their mission and I am grateful. They wished to save my soul, in this world or the next, and they tried tirelessly. Mercy is wasted on evil and they were merciless. And I am grateful.

I was lonely and never alone. There were voices. They spoke on religious matters, on matters of right and wrong and I learnt, and I imagined a world outside these twenty-six paces. They gave me a book with many words. It is about time and right and wrong. And magic.

Time is nothing to me. I have floor and walls and ceiling and food and the cycle of my body. My body has grown and I am near a man. I do not know how to say that in years, but it is many - five or fifty or five hundred. My body has grown and I should be weak. I know no sun, nor air. I am fed little and eat less. They tell me evil rejects food. Demons turn it to poison and my stomach churns. It is all part of my correction. And I am grateful.

But I am evil. This is my testament. I feel lucid and clear. They burnt me today and I felt it rise. Rage, uninhibited and arrogant, drowns sense and fear. Rage consumes me and I remember nothing but fury. And I beat them and I broke them - rage as I've never known - and now they are no more and I am evil and I am ungrateful and I will never be saved. And they are no more. And they are nothing. And I am alone. And I am no-one other than my father's son. And I am my father's son, nameless and ungodly. And the door is open. And I am alive.

MRS CAROLINE BRYCE

"The kid's ok. They'll keep him in a couple of days but he'll be fine."

"Poor little shit. Some fucking people. She'll be regretting that second glass."

"Think so? I'm not sure. You can smell the entitlement."

"She's had some time to stew. D'you want to wait for the brief?

"No. Fuck it. Let's find out what she's got to say."

They let themselves into an interview room. A woman sitting at the table snivelling into a handkerchief.

"Mrs Bryce? Thank you for your patience. We're aware that this is difficult. It's important you understand how serious this is. We advise complete co-operation."

"Yes, yes, of course. I'm so terribly sorry. Is he ok?"

"We're not sure yet. Fingers crossed."

Sobs - expensive make-up running.

"Mrs. Bryce. We'll be recording this interview. I point your attention to the use of a new tape. I'm Detective Inspector Robert Doulon. This is Detective Sergeant Natalie Cargill. This interview is commencing at 23.56 on the 19th July 2019.

Would you please announce yourself for the tape Mrs. Bryce?"

Splutters through the sobs, "Mrs Caroline Bryce."

"Ok Mrs Bryce. Calm down. If you could tell us your date of birth, your address and then just walk us through what happened."

...

Caroline air kisses Therese and taps her pin into the machine. She wraps her pashmina, throws her card into her bag, downs the last of her wine. It's warm - mid-Summer. Rosé-grey, still light at 9, the drizzle that's started welcome relief from the congealing humidity.

A brief, graceless moment as she drops her keys, scrabbles to pick them up. The filth of the pavement. Then the leather-finish safety of the car.

A moment to choose what to listen to. Turn it up.

Out towards Fulham, past Stamford Bridge - a quick thought of her husband in his loathsome, too-tight, blue shirt. Over the river. Nothing remarkable. No incident. Right off Dolmar Hill.

Someone texts. Caroline checks who it is, then cancels - she knows better than to type whilst driving. It's only Therese. Turn onto Caulfield Road. Then Therese calls - she must've left something. The phone's loud, shrill through the car speakers. Falteringly, Caroline silences it. The music's paused - Ace of Base. Clumsy fingers. One look to press play again. The music comes back on much too loud. Caroline stabs at the phone, silences it...

BANG!

Something hits her windscreen. She misses what, just a flash going over the top of her and a cave of smashed glass. She stops. Panic. Caroline welded to her seat. A glimpse in the mirror. Something - a pile of limbs - motionless in the road behind her.

It's quiet - empty. No one around. The sun's dipped below the horizon, bleeding, muddy-pink, onto the bottom of the clouds. No one's out in the suburbs. There are no cameras. Caroline should know - she was part of the committee that has been lobbying for more surveillance in the area. She could carry on. She could park in the garage, take it to the mechanic first thing. Maybe it's fine.

God, how awful. She takes a deep breath and forces another look in her rear-view. She needs the glass - a filter. To turn and see anything directly is too real, too horrifying. It's still in the middle of the right hand lane: non-descript, lifeless.

Caroline calls 999. Police and ambulance. She's out of the car, looking at the damage, impotent - anything to delay acknowledging what's behind her. The windscreen and the crushed metal a surrealist smudge from bonnet to wing above the front wheel.

An operator is trying to calm her down.

Terrified, she approaches the figure, every step convulses her. The operator asks for vital signs - pulse, breathing, blood - but Caroline doesn't know any of that. Hyperventilating. Heart thumping. Hysteria knocking. She touches lightly, then with a little more pressure. Skin's waxy, pale. The operator's asking for vital signs. Caroline sways over the chasm of panic. The body's still warm - she checks for breathing. Limbs are scrawny and limp. The body responds, passive, flopping, head lolling with her touch. It's a child. Maybe ten years old. Caroline collapses in the middle of the road as another car pulls up. The driver jumps out and the police arrive and…

…

Heaving sobs.

"We'll be right back Mrs Bryce".

They step out, gravitate towards the coffee machine.

"Is this worth it? No one's pressing charges. The kid's fine. We should just put her out of her misery and send her on her way. She was a fraction over. She won't be if we breathalyse her again."

"Hmmm? Maybe you're right. We still need to work out who the kid is…"

Back into the interview room. Caroline's red-eyed, exhausted. They give her a cup of tea.

"Mrs Bryce. Some good news. It looks like the child'll make a full recovery. There're no charges being brought against you, for the moment. Operating a vehicle over the legal alcohol limit is incredibly serious, regardless of how small the amount. We're showing lenience in this instance. Against standard procedure."

"Thank you. I know. I know. I'm so, so sorry. I only had one glass…"

"Before we let you go, Mrs Bryce, I just want to ask if you can run through the moment of the crash and the immediate aftermath one more time."

"We still haven't been able to ascertain who the child is, or where he came from. Perhaps there's something you've forgotten - might be a tiny detail - but anything at all that could help us."

"I don't know. It was all so fast. I just remember seeing a flash of something to my right…"

Sobs, snorts.

There's a plan of the scene on the table - an aerial shot with the accident marked, notes scrawled - red lines and arrows.

"I think that's where he came from. From the houses on this side, rather than the estate."

"Which house? This one?"

"I don't know, I wasn't looking. I'm sure he came from the right though. The windscreen was smashed right in front of me, on the driver's side. The dent's on the right."

"Take a guess. If you had to pick one house he might've came out of."

She points at the house just ahead of the car.

"But I didn't see it. Just the direction."

"Is there anything else?"

More sobs, more heaves. She shakes her head.

"OK. Thank you, Mrs Bryce. We appreciate your co-operation."

They walk Mrs Bryce to reception. Her husband's waiting.

"Could someone bloody tell me what's going on?"

More sobbing.

"Bye Mrs Bryce."

"Please don't leave the country for the next few weeks - active investigation and all that."

Mrs Bryce and her husband go,

"Jesus Caz. What the fuck happened?"

"A bit strong?"

"Huh?"

"All that 'Don't leave the country… A bit much?"

"Maybe. I didn't like her - snooty cow. Got away with murder." Cargill laughing, "We going to the house?"

LYNDON

What happened? You tell me what happened. What happened to my wife? You want me to tell you? There's nothing to tell. My wife's afraid. She don't want to come back. No story. I'll tell you what Grace told me, then *you* tell *me* what happened.

Grace said that Bed 7 went into cardiac arrest at 11.40. She said she came back from break to bedlam. The boy died on the ward in the worst kind of way - defibrillator, oxygen, convulsing and screaming. Some of the children, she said, even with sedatives and pain-killers and sickness, were howling. Just kids, scared.

You know fear? Fear's somebody just like you dying, right there, right next to you. You're powerless, and worse, so's everybody else. Poor kids. Not even ten and every day they're reminded that they're dying, that there's nothing they can do. Grace breaks her heart every day for those kids. Everyone that loves them and has told them that it'll be OK, everyone, including Grace, is lying. My wife has to deal with that every single day. And it's hard, you know?

And now this.

Gracie said most of them were too sick to wake, even with all the bawling and banging. In fits and coughs and groans they all fall asleep again. By one, the ward's silent.

Grace does her checks - everything quiet, everything as it should be. She settles down at her desk to write her reports.

The orderly goes on break at 2.15. Gracie's still doing her admin - it's when she gets the most done, when the ward's quiet and everyone's sleeping - no distractions. She's tired and the work's mindless. It's a relief from the shift, a moment to be still and quiet. She remembers the hiss and beep of life being supported - peaceful, she said.

Then a noise she doesn't recognise - humming or gurgling. Grace ignores it - it's a machine, or the air-conditioning, or the orderlies outside. Then it changes. She hears words, but no words that she knows, no language she recognises, and she hears them all there. Grace speaks a little Polish, a little Urdu, some Twi, but she doesn't recognise this. She pulls herself up - she's tired and stiff and a grandma to five babies. She follows the sound. The words are stone, she said - they grate and scratch, you know? Grace says she felt afraid, out of nowhere, like a prickle, you know? It's out of character too. Grace is a tough woman. She's raised four children, seen them grow and prosper, have their own kids. She's grown up a black, British woman in the 70s and 80s. She was born here and lord knows she's seen the worst of people…But this, this sound, like speaking in tongues, she said. This has her scared.

She says the ward's always so familiar, but it changed. She knew it wasn't anything real, but she felt a chill. She said she felt all the hurt. The voice didn't get louder, just clearer maybe. Bed 5. The child had been run over. She said he was a strange boy. He showed no pain. He stayed silent even when she took blood. She hadn't noticed him all night, even with the commotion earlier. Now this kid's sitting up, speaking tongues. Speaking to Grace. She didn't understand anything he said. He was blank - not scared, not in pain, not angry. Just… Just blank. Grace said maybe he was speaking Italian, but it didn't sound like any Italian she knew. It sounded like gibberish.

Now Grace is afraid. She wants to help the boy, check his charts and comfort him, but she felt like she was under water, moving through a swamp, or glue. Scared, you understand? She said it was like the boy was wearing a mask - she couldn't sense happy or sad or good or bad.

Grace tried to soothe the kid, tried to show she wasn't a threat. She tried to make him stop speaking because the words were scaring her, and she doesn't know why. She said he was blank - nothing behind his eyes, you understand? Just staring and the words. And she knows the words were bad. She knows when she hears violence. She knows just by the sound that something was wrong. She said it was like tasting something sour.

She took the boy's hand, and nothing. For a moment he was still. She said he fell quiet, the last few words getting softer, his mouth moving, like he was chewing, until he's just staring at her. Scrutinising her, you know? Gracie smiled. She forced herself calm, forced down the tremble in her hand.

She doesn't know what happened, but the boy screamed, loud and painful, right in her face, and jumped backwards out of the bed, as though Grace had hurt him. Then the kid ran away, on all fours. Like a dog. Gone.

She told me all this and told me to tell you, and she hasn't said another word since. So now you tell me what's happening. Tell me something I can tell my wife. Tell me something to stop my Gracie feeling scared. Please.

SOCO MARK CLEPPER

It's clearing out. Less stampeding plod. He'll have a fag then one more look downstairs, on his own, once the photographer's out the way.

He's been sat against the wall for an hour writing his report. Discomfort - sharp pains through his coccyx, the familiar ache in his knee - falling apart.
It's raining. Mark lights a cigarette, inhales, watching the circus of a crime scene peter out. Hangover's kicking in. Supposed to be a day off.

Only two cars left alongside his, one marked - the coppers guarding the place - the other must be the dickhead photographer's. A loud, bright red BMW Z3 - a hairdresser's motor. He walks round the house, down the side-return to the garden. Another look at the little window that rests on the floor. It was hidden, half way down, behind a garden hose and a wheelbarrow. The window frame's still there, but the glass has been removed, the cavity filled with cement. Inside, all the hardware's been removed so you'd never know there'd been a window. It's a shit job - slap dash, untidy. Mark kicks it, crouches, making sure there's nothing that might be worth his attention, no silver-bullet clues, no case-winning evidence. There's not. Just concrete and weeds.

Mark flicks his fag at the photographer's car, satisfaction when the stub lands on the fabric hood, burning defiant against the rain. Here he comes. The photographer struggles out of the house with his gear - two Peli-cases, a soft bag (maybe the lights that took up so much fucking space?) and a tripod. Mark watches him drop the tripod, fumble everything else to pick it back up. The warm glow of someone else's suffering. Or this prick's specifically. He makes it another couple of steps closer to his car and drops the tripod again.

Mark snaps from his dazed contempt, ashamed - be bigger, be better. He hurries across and sweeps up what he can, forcing charm.

"You want a hand?"

The photographer confused - he must've seen Mark watching him struggle. Polite surliness as Mark tries to help load the cases into the boot, the photographer thanking him, but unloading the case Mark's loaded to start again.

Mark bites his lip - says nothing. Instead, he stands there, vacant, distracted by a wave of nausea, bile seeping onto his tongue, a dehydrated tingling in his fingers. The photographer climbs behind the wheel and reverses out of the drive. Mark, waving mindlessly, elsewhere. Anxiety rises with nausea. Shame. Guilt. The car pulls out and Mark catches himself, drops his arm to his side and shoots a quick, self-conscious glance around to see who saw.

A new set of latex gloves. The sensory gratification of the rubber. The smell and tautness as he fights against friction to get his fingers comfortable. Flashes - fingers in his mouth, a condom choking him, stubble scratching his shoulder, the briefest flutter of pheromones and diving, pleading into helplessness as he pushes him down. Shake that off. Mark descends, back into the cellar.

It's dirty, dark, but it was once a bright, white box - surgical. Poured concrete floors painted white, whitewashed walls in the bedroom, ancient white tiles in the bathroom. Spots in the ceiling are the only light fixtures, the only switch in the corridor is outside the door. All but one of the bulbs have gone. The lighting alone would have Mark killing someone if he had to stay down there.

Click! Mark gets it. The room's a cell. How's no-one seen it? Locks and light switches outside, reinforced door. The room's a fucking cell.

Mark pacing, seeing through new eyes. He's on the floor in the bathroom, oblivious of the grime, on his side with a torch trying to see behind the sink, behind the toilet. He's back in the bedroom, tapping the wall, kicking the skirting board. When he can't find anything, he's back trying the tiles in the bathroom, laboured, tapping each one. He finds a loose one, jimmies and shifts it. Nothing. No idea what he's looking for, but anything…A sign. A message from the past.

Memory of an old job. Four young girls found dead, locked in a shipping container. There'd been over 70 people in the container. Sixty-six escaped and disappeared and are now trying to make lives for themselves somewhere, or fighting deportation, or taking on the gruelling journey out of whatever hell they've been returned to.

Four girls' bodies, and the filth and detritus of too many people locked in a metal box for too long. The girls documented their last days - a macabre diary, written in Pashtun, scratched into the green paint on the walls. He still has the translation, one phrase burnt into his memory: "I see death and there is no peace".

Humans don't die quietly, they go out full-voiced, kicking and screaming, clawing at life, desperate to share their pain, desperate to be heard. Even with no voice, the instinct is to communicate.

Mark taps a tile in the corner over the shower tray - a different sound. Pressure on the bottom corner pivots the opposite side away from the wall. He can get a finger behind to remove it. There's a cavity. He's got his head on the floor, his torch poking light into the hollow. There's a slip of paper and a small toy.

He takes photographs, covering all angles, showing the position of the cavity, the items within, the tile cover. He opens an evidence bag and finds his tweezers.

His heart's racing. That familiar conflict - excitement versus horror - the elation of knowing he's discovered something important, tempered by the knowledge that he's inching closer to truth, and in truth, closer to some terrible suffering.

The scrap of paper's ripped from a book. There's one line of tiny print:

"Ego patrem filius expertibus, ossibus molitis, et impii."

The print's hand-written, printed - Roman type - like the font of a book. Look closer. The letters aren't quite regular, the line of text not quite straight. It's been scratched rather than printed, using dirt and water, or blood. Like a stick-and-poke tattoo. Mark bags it, seals it.

Then the toy, a tiny little figurine, like the little lead soldiers Mark used to leave around the house for his father to tread on. Except this is wood. Hand-carved, rough, someone using fingernails or teeth, or a sharpened stone. It's a small boy - the scale and perspective near perfect, but the child has enormous wings bursting from his back and arms much longer than they should be, taloned, spikes for fingers. The wings are covered in scratches that might be words, but Mark can't make them out.

Behind the toy, at the back of the cavity: a pile of milk teeth, still flecked with blood. Mark counts them into a bag - seventeen. He can't remember how many kids lose.

Phhhnk! The last bulb blinks out. The room's a void, a vacuum, before what little light leaks from the stairway penetrates the gloom, softens the edges. Mark shudders, turns his torch on to bag up the teeth.

Quick check - everything as it should be, torch-light scanning for anything he's forgotten. The darkness is muddied. Shadows have taken on a new threat, suffocating. He runs the last half of the stairs, a child's sense of being followed.

ALEXANDRA CLAY

"Here we go. Remember: flat and even and firm - "NO COMMENT". Every question, without hesitation or emotion. You understand?"

Nothing.

Here they are. DI Tweedle and PC Dum.

"I'm Detective Inspector Robert Doulon. This is Detective Sergeant Cargill. We'll be recording this and although you haven't been charged as yet, what you say will be on the record and can be used as evidence."

Jesus Christ. So serious.

"Thank you detective."

Handshakes all round. Smiles. Charm. Fucking idiots.

"We'd like to ask you some questions…"

Yeah… Yeah, he's checking how it's spelt.

"Mr dee Blight?"

"Mr *de Bligt* will be happy to co-operate as far as he can, Mr Doulon."

"Will Mr *di Bleek* be speaking at all for himself this afternoon?"

He's got teeth. How exhausting.

"Certainly. Mr de Bligt, are you comfortable? Do you need anything?"

Dead. Nothing. Maybe he's comatose - a high functioning catatonic.

"Hello Thomas. Could we start with you giving us your name, date of birth and address?"

Is he going to respond? Nope. There's the look from the sidekick. Smile - yeah. Fuck off. He's legitimately brain-dead. Not my problem.

"Name, date of birth and address?"

Nope, nothing.

"Ms Clay? Will your client be answering any questions?"

"My client hopes to be as co-operative as he possibly can be, Mr Doulon."

"Name, date of birth and address?"

"No comment."

Ah. Hello Tommy.

"Could you tell us where you were on the 19th July 2019?"

"No comment."

The old rope-a-dope. Shake off that brain-damage.

"Tell us who did this to you. Who put you in hospital, Thomas?"

"No comment"

"What were you doing in the basement of no. 15 Caulfield Road on the 19th July?"

"No comment."

"No? Don't remember? Some officers found you unconscious in the basement, next to a dead woman. Ms Gabrielle Solano? Ring any bells?"

"No comment."

"How do you know Gabrielle?"

"No comment."

"Was Ms Solano your lover?"

"No comment."

He's persistent this chap. Good for him.

"Who owns the house? We looked into it and the only thing we know for sure is that it's not you or Ms Solano."

"No comment."

"Have you been living there?"

"No comment."

"Did Ms Solano live there?"

"No comment."

"What's the basement used for?"

"No comment."

"Is the basement used as a cell, Thomas?"

Was that a twitch, Tom?

"No comment"

"Were you keeping someone prisoner?"

"No comment."

Hold it together you piece of shit. I saw you flinch. What nastiness are you hiding?

"There's a lot of blood down there - a real mess."

Fuck's sake. What else?

"Are you involved in human trafficking, Mr de Bligt?"

"No comment."

"Who were you keeping down there? Was it a young boy?"

Jesus.

"No comment"

"Who is he?

"No comment."

"He's gone missing. Where would he have gone?"

Keep it even-keeled, Tommo, you fucking nonce.

"No comment."

"This is fucking pointless..."

I don't think that's procedure... And on tape. Tsk tsk.

"Thomas de Bligt, we're arresting you on suspicion of kidnap, human trafficking and murder. Anything you do..."

Murder? Bollocks. What's happened? Just like that?

"My client has prepared a statement that he has asked I read..."

"What?"

"A statement."

"Quickly."

So tetchy. Big smile. Three, two…

"'My name is Thomas Karla de Bligt. I am 42 years old. I am from Utrecht, but I have been in the UK for 17 years. I work as an electrician and I am a faithful and loyal servant of God. I have been in the service of God's plan to save us for over 10 years and no-one may judge me but God. I have already lost countless work hours and suffered much physical and psychological trauma…'"

Let's edit… Jesus. The ramblings of a mad man… Oh, no. No. Completely batshit. Cut. Edit.

"'Only God can save me and only service to the church can win you God's favour. In the name of the Father, the Son and the Holy Spirit. The work that we have been doing is of the utmost important. Understand this, show mercy and release me back to the Lord's ordained mission.'"

Yup. I know. Retarded. I agree. Just doing my job.

"Thank you for that. If there's nothing else? No? OK.

We're arresting you on suspicion of kidnap, human trafficking and murder. Anything you do say can, and will, be taken as evidence and can, and will be used in a court of law against you."

"You will be removed to a private room whilst you recover and until we move you to remand."

A private room - every cloud…

"Do you understand?"

"No comment."

Boom, boom! Such wit. We might still learn to get along, Thomas.

GABRIELLE

No light. No space. Weightless enormity. Dense nothingness. Gliding, falling, floating. Sinking, crushing, squeezing. Streaks of time, love, guilt. Streams of memory, touch, smell, arousal, but snaking away, carrying it away, flowing, portals to there. Slowing to a trickle. Separation. Broken into a galaxy of pieces, spread across all that there is. Atomised. Everything all at once. Everything the same in structure and matter and cell and particle. Atomise everything. Everything as nothing. Nothing then. Nothing now. Nothing. Blackness. Loneliness. Isolation. Connection, to everything, everyone. Every heartbeat, every tide, every final exhalation. Every cut, burn and suffocation. Electricity. And it suffocates. And it fills, scorching through, intertwined with anything, everything, everyone, everywhere. Warmth. Comfort. Inclusion. Faith. Trust. Disappointment. Anger. Pain. Infinities of sorrow. Infinities of time. Infinity. Infinity. In finality. Final. The end. No more. No future. No past. No now. Know now. Know all. All knowledge. All knowing. All conscious - unbounded awareness. No memory. No me. No you. No mass. No consciousness. No conscience. No being. No self. Just energy. Just sorrow. Everything is linked. Everything is important. Everything is nothing. Nothing matters. Nothing mattered. No good. No bad. No right. No wrong. Just energy and connection and pain and joy and your pain and your joy and my pain and my regret and my guilt and my sorrow and my pain and my regret and my guilt and my sorrow and pain and regret and guilt and sorrow and regret and guilt and sorrow and regret and guilt and sorrow and guilt and sorrow and guilt and sorrow and guilt and sorrow and guilt and sorrow and guilt and sorrow and guilt and sorrow and sorrow and sorrow and sorrow and sorrow and sorrow and sorrow and sorrow and sorrow and sorrowsorrowsorrowsorrowsorrowsorrowsorrowsorrowsorrowsorrowsorrowsorrowsorrowsorrow.

CHILD

The scent surges across the pack from the side. We bank in the direction of the wind and it fills our nostrils and we run, and it's straight ahead of us. Not far now. The scent sits right below where the giant white face rests its chin on land and we run towards it, and we bark, and we stop and he howls, and she howls, and I howl and we all howl at the white face, but it ignores us. It refuses to meet our eye, looks off to another horizon as though we don't howl at it. And we howl at it. And the scent tugs. And we run.

We run. We run on snow and ice, and it's silent. We run on grass, lush and green and it springs and gives us more speed. We run through mud and across streams and rivers and we mask our scent and we lose anyone behind us, but we never lose the scent, even as it shifts and twists, it clings to our nose and calls to us.

And we're hungry and we answer the call and we run and we run and the scent gets stronger and the moon's white face gets bigger and bigger and brighter. And the night behind grows thicker and bluer and I see the white face repeated as a ghost when I look back into dark, but it's faint and what I really see is the scent, winding, coiling towards us and past us and around us and what we see is the scent, and it's stronger now and twisting and holding in the wind and we're connected to it. It flows through us, through each nose and out again on breath and spit and I can see it broken, but so strong that it never breaks and keeps moving behind us. And the white face beams, and it's bright as day ahead and dark and cold as hell behind. It's the land of the dead, and we're following the scent and it's close. And we are one.

...

I was nursed by dogs. They told me this. Raised by wild dogs and I was feral and I have the memory of how to run and track and scavenge burnt into me. The howls of wolves fill my sleep. Before memory I was this and my body remembers.

And I have run and run and the world is bigger than it can be and there is much I don't know and I run and I run and I run. And there are others and they are bigger and they are many and they sway and they shout and they stare.

And I run and there are machines of glass and metal that move faster than I run and they consume others, but not me. And I run. And I run from machines and I run past giants and they shout and everyone is bigger and everything is bigger and it is loud and there is much I don't understand.

But I was a dog before I was a boy and I can run and track and scavenge. And I am the son of my father and we are nameless and ungodly, and I was chosen to do great things, and I was a dog once and I can follow the scent and I can find my father and I can see him for the demon he is and I will have no mercy, for mercy is wasted on evil and I will right the wrong and I will be corrected.

And I run and I run. And dark turns to light and I see the sun and she burns and she blinds and she is glorious and I have never imagined anything so bright and I run from her, but she follows, flying high above, getting further away, but never letting me go, heating my back so I know she's there. And there are more people and more machines and I run and there are fewer buildings, and I run, and there are more trees and green and less grey and stone. And I run and I run until I cannot and then I sleep, on the grass, under the sun, with the wind and the sounds and the scents.

...

Awake. The sun rising and the world is pink and hazy and warm and there is a mist rolling and water hangs on the grass by my head, each blade carrying a single drop. But I am tired and my eyes are not ready to open and I am not safe and I can feel them near and I try to move, to rise, keep moving, to find safety, but I cannot. I cannot move my neck. I cannot move my hands. I cannot move my legs or toes. I am imprisoned in sleep. My own body punishes me, for I am evil and I have much work to do. And I can feel them drawing closer and I know that scent and I know that it is pain and terrible and all-consuming. And I know that I am important and that I will make a difference to the world and that I must suffer but must not die. And they draw closer and I can feel the rumble of their breath, and I can smell it, acrid and foul, and they're close and over me but I cannot move. I try to scream and the scream fills my chest and head, but will not break from my lips and I know fear and the evil looms, casting a shadow and I cannot turn to meet them and I cannot move and I cannot scream and it starts to rain, or is it drool, and I wait for death and the rain grows heavier…

...

And I'm awake and I can move and my fear was a nightmare and nightmares have followed me into the world. Rain falls in waves and I am soaked and cold. And I am free. I am free.

IVY WITHERS
Camilla Grudova

The first place Charles and I lived in together was an ice cream truck. The wheels were removed. It sat on cement blocks. It had a complicated kitchen, all sorts of slots for ice cream cones, taps which nothing came out of, and no hot plate or toaster. On the side was a painting of an anthropomorphic ice cream, with cherry eyes and beige limbs, surrounded by tiny dancing popsicles with big eyelashes. The truck played Beethoven's *Fur Elise* using the mysterious fixture on the truck top. Charles fixed it so it went off every morning. We used it as our alarm clock. I said how funny, to write a song about a hairy girl, and Charles told me it meant something else in a foreign language.

In the kitchen's strange little compartments, we put things that didn't belong. Stuffed here and there were the forgotten dunce hats of snow cones. Under the driver's seat, we found bottles of congealed syrup, in yellow, blue, red, orange. We loved the colour so much. It gave Charles the idea to dye his hair orange, though his scalp didn't have much more hair than an arm. The dye he bought was gone after two baths and one rainfall. It was a cheap dye called Orange Blossom Prince, I think.

Just after we moved into the truck, we saw a hot air balloon shaped like a two faced clown, one face was blue, the other pink and yellow. Both with a laughing grin. We used a ladder to climb onto the roof to see it better, we didn't have binoculars, but we could see the flame, pouff pouff! "A Magician!" I said. The truck roof creaked underneath us. "There will be dents," Charles scowled and we climbed down again.

A policeman came and told us the ice cream truck wasn't a legal or sanitary house and we had to leave.

Our new home was a former Baptist church, a small grey building without a steeple we broke into. It had two floors. On the first floor was where the congregation met, there was a long hall with a stage, and on the stage, a pool with a trap door, used to baptize people. The pool was white inside, with steps leading down, and did not have any drain. I was doubtful it could hold water without leaking. We stayed on the second floor, where the pastor used to live. It had green and black linoleum floors, and two bathtubs, one smaller than the other. All the drawers in the kitchen were full of mouse droppings, and there was no stove. There was a dreadful mattress - stains of tea, blood, soup &c. It was too heavy to carry down the stairs so we took all the stuffing out, and put the bags out one by one along with the empty skin of the mattress.

There were lots of signs with religious writings on them still on the walls. I preferred stained glass to words, but this church had no stained glass.

I remember once going to an Anglican church which had a reproduction of William Holman Hunt's "Light of the World" except backwards, Jesus on the other side than he is in the painting, behind the glass there was an electric light, which the church turned on in the evenings, for passersby to see. All the other windows around the church were the colour of lemon flavoured jelly, the kind served to sick children in hospitals.

We had only been living in the Baptist church a few weeks when Charles' cousin Ivy showed up. I had never met her, but Charles had told me about her. She often came up in conversation when Charles discussed his own hair loss. "My Cousin Ivy" he said, "her hair was the same colour as mine, but it went white at some point, and she started to dye it black rather than its original colour."

She didn't have much luggage: a very small black velvet knapsack which was very wrinkled, and a round hat box with stripes on it.

We didn't have any extra bedding but a little brown tent Charles had lived in before the ice cream truck. We set it up and comfortably filled it with jumpers and socks, but she took the poles out of the tent and lay it flat, sleeping on it like nest. After the first night, she moved it upstairs to where we were, saying the pool was evil.

Charles thought we should fill the pool with pillows or plastic balls like in the play areas of hamburger restaurants but that somehow seemed dangerous to me. I imagined one of us suffocated underneath them.

"Here's a thing about Ivy", Charles whispered to me after we had gone to bed. "She used to stand on the sidewalk and say hello to men who walked by, they all shunned her and looked away but she would keep on standing there saying hello."

Ivy wore a pair of brown, imitation leather boots with laces, they were warped out of shape, like wood exposed to moisture, the tips curved upwards so she looked like a hobgoblin, and struggled to walk in them.

Ivy's hair was all straight and fine at the front, but dreadfully tangled behind her ears. I didn't understand how such lank, dyed hair could tangle, but it sat on the back of her neck like a well-fed spider. Ivy re-dyed her hair in our bathroom, leaving marks everywhere that resembled black feathers or mould.

Everything she owned had small printed stickers with her name and address on it. They were a gift from a mutual uncle who worked in an office, she said, and so had access to such things - name stickers, envelopes, scissors, paperclips. Ivy had blacked out the address however, as it was her childhood address, so it simply read:

Ivy Withers

One of her labelled possessions was a taxidermy turtle - the legs and head were stuffed and the shell was covered in some sort of shellac so it was really shiny. She kept it in a biscuit tin, wrapped up in a scarf. Another was a potato she seemed to have no intention of eating - nor did she offer it to us for our hospitality. Instead, she often took it out of her hatbox as an excuse to tell a vulgar story about a gentleman who put potatoes in his swimsuit.

She had three outfits. A stiff, cream linen dress with stains on it, a black satin dress with holes under the armpits, and a green dress.

For menstruation, she had a dark, red cup thing that resembled an anatomical heart. She left it in the bathroom half full of syrupy blood.

Charles and I both worked in a plant store, that is how we met. The store had ferns in glass containers, small palm trees, certain plain types of cactuses, green hens-and-chicks, grasses. No flowers, it was not a florist's. Everything was green and brown. We tended to the plants, and delivered them to houses, Charles had a cart attached to a bicycle with which to deliver them, there was a tiny maroon truck the store owner used to use to make deliveries, but now it was broken, and sat in the backyard of the store with its wheels removed.

We had a small tree from the plant store. Ivy ate it, including the leaves and branches, so we decided never to invite her to our work.

Charles wasn't surprised. He told me that one Christmas their grandmother gave her an encyclopaedia of seaweed, with real seaweed samples in it. Ivy peeled them out and ate them like crisps, leaving pale brown glue shadows on the pages. Their grandma also gave her a pink parasol and a box of quail eggs, Charles said.

Ivy accumulated things, but not bags or cases to put them in. A stack of Raggedy Ann picture books, a black umbrella with Mickey Mouse on it, a child sized chest of drawers with giraffes and mice painted on it, a mannequin's hand, a clown doll with a gold sequined costume with a black feather frill and cuffs, a carpet with a pattern of yellow roses, a number of chipped cups with letters on them: L, B, A, C, three lamps which she placed on top of our drawers without plugging them in.

She made a nice little corner for herself in our church. She never swept it, the bottom of her feet or her stockings were grey.

She stole my favourite polka dot dress, and wore it every day, spelling tea on it and sweating the arms, but not my olive coloured baseball cap. I stopped taking it off even when I went to bed, just in case she took an interest in it, I hoped she would think it was an unremovable part of my body, some sort of moss like thing.

She took my yellow *Sweet's Anglo-Saxon Reader In Prose And Verse* and carried it around under her arm. She left a Raggedy-Ann scratch and sniff book on Charles and I's bed, as if in exchange. All the scents that were supposed to smell like different things inside the book just smelt like mildew.

She found three toy animals: a lion, a horse, and a moose, made with real animal skin and hair, the lion was missing a patch, you could see the white plastic underneath, they were most likely made from old horses, Charles told us, that their insides were made into glue and their outsides into toys like these. The knowledge deranged her somehow, despite her taxidermied tortoise, which I think she truly believed still had some life in it. She mock fed it bits of lettuce and leaves before eating the greens herself.

We took her to this toyshop that had a stained glass window depicting snow white and the seven dwarves. We loved it because it was so colourful, though there was cardboard over one of the dwarves' faces as it was cracked, and someone had drawn something wicked where his face was supposed to be. Ivy said "That's what I want. Seven tiny men to look after me. They'll make me pancakes and wash my stockings." She tried to walk into the window, I pulled on the back of her dress. Charles explained to her that it was just a window, not a real life opportunity. She thought we were tricking her and didn't speak to us for days. She stuck our forks and our socks in the toilet.

"Ivy once had a boyfriend," Charles told me, "a man who didn't shun her when she said hello. His name was Thomas, he looked like an umbrella because of the triangular shape of the coat he wore, and the black cap always on his head. He poisoned himself to death by swallowing a cupful of appleseeds."

It took me a whole day to fill the baptismal pool, carrying pots back and forth. I did it on a day Charles was at work and I wasn't. I thought I should drown Ivy before she killed us, as I believed she'd killed Thomas herself, or had convinced him to eat all those appleseeds.

When she saw that I had filled the pool, Ivy took off all of her clothes except for her underpants and jumped in, as I had wanted. She didn't dunk her head under, just swam back and forth - it only took two strokes each way. I had no idea how I would empty it. The same way I filled it, I suppose. When Ivy was swimming in the other direction from me and I couldn't see her face, I shut the trap door on her, then ran upstairs before I could hear anything.

IT'S NICE WHEN TIME STOPS
Augustin Cambau

This is a cis-heterosexual man with no pronoun preferences who lives on a territory that is part of what was once called France, on an island just off a bit of coast that sticks out of the mainland like a handless arm. This is near the end of Europe, and the end of time still; it hasn't ceased being the end of time for a few centuries now. The end-times are now a state of being, though of course one that doesn't ever stop changing. This territory is still called Normandy, and centred around the city of Rouen, deep inland. He is far from this nucleus of the territory, in the countryside; there are far more plants than human beings here, more plants than humans and the things they build. A lot has gone to waste, among the useless things that people built at the beginning of the end of time, when acceleration was the only type of motion capable of maintaining together the loose limbs and coverings of the machines they called France, Europe, the West, the Economy. People these days wonder at all the things that people felt compelled to do back then. Sometimes they envy them. But then the most perceptive among them remember again the discomfort that dribbled down off the backs of the previous generation, and of all the generations between that time and this time, till now, though it is now just a drizzle, a habit, and intuition whispers that what is now a drizzle of discomfort must've been a river once, a sea; these people from the beginning of the end-times were quite probably drenched in this, this muscle-drying and eye-tiring lack of comfort. How then to feel envy? Things are more calm now. That wave has crashed.

When this man (he usually wears a common masculine French-culture name) looks out from where he likes to sit in the morning, towards the sea and the mainland, he sees the hill the house he lives in has been built upon, receding down and down into more and more shrubs, more and more trees and at the bottom sandhills, and behind those, the sea. At this hour, his child might be playing within his gaze, squatting between the shrubs, among the low plants that grow there. People here have favoured some over others, but for the most part they let them be, just take what's needed for food and day-to-day medicine.

This child is a playful one, with tiny legs and tiny arms. The trees look huge by comparison. At this time of the morning, the child might also be in the house, watched by others, but he'd still be able to hear their laughter and piercing screams of excitement. He usually enjoys the screams and the laughter but right now they are distracting him; he's trying to think of a story for them (them: the child. These days people tend to use neutral language about children till they choose an identity they enjoy, though they can change anytime they wish to. Not everyone does this, but most people do.), at bedtime, or on the sandhills above the beach, ideally; he wants the story to be about mermaids. Sirens. (Stories are important to him and others, most others it seems, and they are a large part of what is swapped in times and places of meeting. They can be from any time or place, indeed they can be invented or changed on the spot, at will; the only rule for stories these days is that they must be worth listening to.)

It has occurred to him (our man) that sirens have human bodies from the head down to the waist, and then long fishtails, and that the human part of their bodies can range from male to female, with everything in between, but that he hadn't till then wondered how they have sex. When he wondered about this, it appeared to him that they could be wholly uninterested in intercourse, like many fish, and simply release eggs and sperm separately when it's time to make babies, but this seemed unsatisfactory to him, and not very relatable. But there had to be an element of holes, that's for sure; if only because there were no legs to separate and reveal some kind of ending at the place of their juncture. It had to be some sort of cavity-thing within the top part of the fish-body. At this time he was considering flaps; flaps were what had occurred to him. Why does he feel the need to explore the anatomy of mythological sea creatures? He doesn't know.

There would be a kind of natural flap of scaly skin, more or less where the pubic area of humans is, and this flap could peel itself back, aggregating into a sort of mound, and then what was under that would be there, quite fishy but also mammalian at the same time. The sex organs can stick out, and be penetrative, or hold themselves inward, with all the sensitive things inside or just barely sticking out, and be receptive. Penetrative-receptive, the classical thing; except in sirens there is the possibility in each individual to either hold their genitals inward, and feel things happen within their flesh, or hold them outwards, and go feel the feeling of other flesh around them. Also these organs can be held at many kinds of in-between points by sexually skilled sirens, and pleasure can be sought through an infinity of games. As for reproduction, like in medieval times, both partners have to feel a spike of watery pleasure to release eggs. The eggs come out and merge. They then fall at the bottom of the sea (in the shallow places where mermaids live), and are either eaten by something, or else grow to become small mermaids. The small mermaids are then either eaten by something, or manage to swim their way back to a group of sirens, who incorporate them into the group and raise them collectively. This idea is pleasing to the man, sitting in his morning sitting place, quite comfortably, with his morning beverage. The trees are bristling in the morning breeze that comes from the sea. Soon it will be time to go inside the land into the forest, and cut down a tree for wood; a woodcutting expedition has been decided on for this day.

Sirens are mammals, like you and I; they have mammary glands. They breathe air, though their huge lungs allow them to stay underwater for almost half an hour. They enjoy the sea, truly; it is their pleasure to swim in it and dive in it, and they find there most of their food. They also enjoy laying their human halves in the sun, on stones or steep beaches (they prefer those to gradually declining beaches), and drinking the sun through their skin. This is where all the salt from the seawater comes out of them, and appears on the skin; they brush it off and feel purified. They like the night-time and the daytime, but have a preference for the night. The rhythm of their lives follows the rhythm of the moon, in its 15-and-15 day cycles. They are a melancholy and quite emotive species, and have a collective fondness for nurturing, caressing and embracing. Like human beings, they take pleasure in stories, and their stories are almost always about truth; they assert truths about the land-places, and the beings that dwell there. They pine about humanity, humans and human ways of living. They also love trees a lot, mostly the idea of trees, and imagine the interactions humans have with them. Big trees are a source of endless fascination for them, and when they see them from afar, they wonder about them, name them, and make up stories about them. They are also proud of being sea-creatures, and belonging to the sea. The sea is the most important thing, it is everything; they derive a kind of self-importance from being part of the juncture between land and sea. They don't care for material technology, and find things clunky; any thing must eventually be released into the sea. What is important is doing the right thing at the right time. Sirens have the privilege of thinking in this way.

The man thinks he's maybe going at excessive lengths to imagine the lifestyle of sirens, and he hasn't yet started to build the story about The Two Sirens Who Were As Twins (but not actual twins); his story is going to be about those two sirens. He knows that they were raised together, and stayed together always, and shunned closeness and love with other members of their groups. From the day that they were tiny little sirens, having broken and swum back up from their eggs at the bottom of the sea, those two became close companions, and everything they learned, they learned together. This the man knows. He also knows they went hunting together always, just the two of them, and ate their food together. The other thing he knows is that during one of their hunts, something happened, and as far as actual storytelling goes, this is what the story will be about.

Then his morning beverage has been drunk, and the sun is going up, and he hears stirring within the house behind him, and he thinks about how the two sirens were very serious beings, extremely serious, much more serious than other sirens were, and the only thing they sought out from others was sex, as they never wished for sex together. As he brought back the empty mug into the kitchen, a large room and always quite tidy, he couldn't keep his mind off just how serious the two sirens were, and their seriousness unnerved him. It occurs to him that the two sirens sought out sex from other sirens in a way that was almost unpleasant, almost just using them, although never absolutely so. In any case, something about those two must've made the others within their group uncomfortable, in the way that people get uncomfortable when something isn't quite right with something. In the main room of the house, right next to the kitchen, the daily tree-cutting party have gathered together, and are speaking about this and that and laughing while they wait. This is a large house that was built in the eighteenth century for a single family and their servants; it now houses around twenty adults and a varying number of children; right now the number must be around fifteen. Some of the children are here now, in the room, interacting with the grown-ups and adolescents; his own child is here, pottering about behind a small wood table that has been painted black with brightly coloured flowers, right in front of one of the large windows through which the morning sun shines bright. On the table there is a printed document about the Progressive Fundamentalists, those people that seek to augment themselves through technologies, of which there are a bunch: psy-tech, bio-tech, infrastructure, spacecraft, self-craft, etc. Specifically, the printed document is about the colonies the Progressive Fundamentalists still have here on earth, where in small numbers they stay and try to optimise things to live the most perfect life. He has read the document over the last few days, and has found himself quite curious and full of wonder at these people and the ways in which they see the world. His child, blissfully unaware, is squatting and sing-songing a litany of two words, while putting things in and out of a small bucket they have in front of them. He feels quite giddy in the present moment, excited and jolly, as he watches his child fooling around between the black lacquered table with its bright flowers, and the wide window through which the sun comes in. He feels compelled to build in his mind a fantasy of his child, having reached the age of twenty, deciding to try and join a colony of Progressive Fundamentalists, as some do, to learn how to build infrastructure or even to join a space-crew to excavate for materials and explore limitless space. The fantasy makes him proud of his imaginary grown-up child, and also disappointed in them for choosing to burden themselves in such a way. He chooses to repel the fantasy, because he knows he wants to keep reeling in the story about The Two Mermaids Who Were As One, or was it As Twins? He can't quite recall.

Then the party sets out, five or six people, carrying sharp axes, long saws, ropes and other woodcutting things, and continuing their conversations as they go out, through the low trees on the land-facing side of the house, and then on between the first flowering trees (it is the very beginning of spring), walking by cultivated gardens and uncultivated spaces that belong to no-one, through the space where no one goes much except children and young people on adventures, the old commercial zone. Here everything is derelict and overrun with exuberant vegetation. The buildings aren't liveable; they can only be used for storage, as some of them, on the outskirts of the area, are; but mostly they are just left to degrade slowly there. The materials they are made from are for the most part not reusable: they are big structures made of welded metal, with wide panels of glass in between and plastic coverings. Or else big boxes made of corrugated sheets of metal. People are just waiting for them to fall apart.

So they walk through this part of their environment, and perhaps some of them try to imagine what this place must've looked like back when it was alive. It must be hard for them, as they have no notion of massive malls, fast-food chains, supermarkets, or even companies and brands in the sense that we define them today. If none of them are historians, they can't begin to fathom what a commerce-driven society really looked like. Maybe one of them is, or has an interest in the subject, and that one has a clearer picture of the events and world-views that led to this place being as it is, and in that case he may be talking as he walks, maybe carrying a bag full of food for the day's lunch, and saying things like "this place is where commerce used to take place, things were made all over the world, and then they were transported to places like this, to be sold for profit. There were places like this all over the territory, in fact all over the world, and they looked very similar to each other, to the point of being quite dreary and boring to those who wrote about them. They were important places, where a lot of time was spent, and yet authors mostly mentioned them only in passing. But when the riots happened, people broke into these places and hoarded the things that were there. We do have a lot of material on that, as most rioters didn't expect to feel the feelings of happiness, and even lust, that they felt as they did the looting and then the sense of despondency and sadness that followed. Many recorded media mention this." And the others might go "ah yes, the riots, we've heard about those", thinking back to the historical event (and emotional toll) they were taught about as adolescents, and not really knowing what the word "riot" could possibly refer to, since in this future time all sense of oppression and class struggle has melted away, along with the ruling class, the economy, and all the things that were a corollary to those. And if you need an explanation for that, mine is that people progressively got fed up after the time of the riots, and started not caring as much about society, governments, and the economy; they were all ruined anyway. So they got to thinking along other lines, and everything just sort of followed from that. It simply happened, collectively, in a long span of time. This explanation is satisfactory at least to me.

If one of the members of the wood-cutting party has a theorizing turn of mind, he may be thinking of what comes next, what this will turn into, since this is the end of time and things just seem to keep fractioning back into simpler things, though technology and science and art are kept preciously - and keep building upon themselves. This person would stop mulling these things over quite fast, as they walked past the old commercial zone and into the woods proper, where it was more interesting to look at trees, plants, and animals. The party have halted at the entrance and one of them (maybe our man), has said something, with some solemnity. Then everyone nodded. Now they are in the forest, walking to a part of the forest where there are big trees that are good now for cutting; this is the last of the tree-cutting that can be done before the sap comes up, as the moon has just begun waning, and by the time it starts a new cycle, spring will probably be too advanced. What little wood they will use this coming spring and summer will mostly be from the day's work.

The man has shut down the story within himself, somewhere inside the region of his stomach. It needs to mature here before it comes out, fully formed; possibly right at the moment when his child will be sat on his lap, in front of the sea, and expecting to hear a good story. It'll need to be ready, truly itself as it should be. It must withstand the child's subsequent questioning and satisfy their instinctual knowledge of what makes a story right. He hopes his will do, because he knows he's trying to communicate something to the child through this story. Right now though, right now is the time for being in the forest, and cutting down the right tree and chopping it up into smaller pieces. The story is baking in the background.

The forest becomes leafier in the beginning of spring, and the sun is shining down from the treetops. Animals can be heard, scurrying under ivy leaves, amid the chattering of birds. Sometimes, below a big tree, the birdsong becomes deafening, a cacophony that pleasantly tickles the top of the brain. Spring time is the best time, the man thinks. He and his companion's bodies are fat and filled with the heat of the winter's fires and rich foods. They want to be naked; or at least he wants to be naked. He wants to fuck. His walk is rather bouncy; flashes of siren anatomy and liquid lovemaking intersperse his noticing of all the forest things around him.

He probably has an ongoing relationship with one or more of the people in the party, or maybe all of his love interests have stayed back home, at the house, or maybe his favourite lover is somewhere else, in another district, witnessing other types of trees, or on top of a brambly hill somewhere, above a big lake that glistens, with strong legs, living things of their own. This is how love happens at the end of time; people usually become more and more monogamous as they age, but they have a healthy respect for their sensual, sexual and emotional appetites. Communities happen, centred usually around places, but sometimes on activities or ways of doing things. People move from one place to the next, or stay in one place, as dictated by their own private reasons. Maybe it is easy to travel fast when it is required, but it is a sacrifice, and still they prefer to travel slowly. They stay in touch through highly advanced forms of distant communication that neither you nor I can fathom. They know the value of being physically near someone, and they know when to shut up. They know what they are doing. As an illustrated example, right now the party have arrived where the trees that are good for firewood are, and they have started weighing the various options and examining the trees. They know how they can make the tree fall, and whether it's any good or not. They feel a small sting as they choose, because one is supposed to feel a sting when one ends something, whatever that thing may be. They are efficient, in that they know by looking at a tree if it's the right tree for their purposes, but they also know to factor other things into their decision for everything to be good and right. They do not suffer from the brain trauma you and I suffer from. They are not too complicated. I would like to be like them.

So then they choose a tree, wonder if it can be cut, and then they set about cutting it. After clearing the moss and things from its foot (feeling a slight sting) they take turns swinging their axes down into its flesh, two people standing next to one another. Then they saw the tree with a long saw, two people, while others just watch and drink water or walk around and gather plants. Then they hammer big metallic triangular things into the cut they have made, and then they saw some more. After a while the tree starts whining and moving, and they know it's going to fall; they scream something, as is done in this moment, and the tree falls down, first slow, then fast; it is held back by its own branches tangling with other branches, but then they break and the tree hits the floor, vibrating throughout the length of its trunk, and for a while they just stand there and watch. Then the ones who were sawing take a rest and eat something, while the others begin preparing to cut it up into smaller logs. A vehicle will arrive at some point in the afternoon to carry the wood back to the house.

A little while later, the man is sitting with his child, on top of a sandhill, in front of the wide blue sea. They are wrapped in a warm blanket that is made from something comfortable and lasting, a good blanket for being outside in the cold evening winds. The child is used to the sea, as they have grown up right in front of it; but still the sight amazes them, and the man also is amazed.

They are silent, till the man starts talking about sirens and the ways in which they live. The child is extremely interested, and asks questions. This is going well. Sirens live in groups. They congregate on rocks. They play in the sea. Their groups are varied in size, individuals move in and out, sometimes they spend some transitional time alone, which is normal. They die from accidents or predation. They mourn their dead. They tell stories while looking to the land. They observe the moon and stars to know cyclical time, and thanks to their understanding of that, they understand space. They like fun and sex, they are both serious and never-serious. They are beautiful to human eyes. Sirens hunt with stealth, patience and collective effort; they use their hands to catch fish and eat it raw. Sirens never cook anything.

He then goes: "there was a time, when in a group of sirens who lived not far from here, two small sirens swam back from the bottom of the ocean on the same day. The first who swam up was called Rea, and the second was called Pon. From that day, they were inseparable. They hunted together, played together, explored the coast together, and learned hunting together from the same adult. Their bond together seemed to engulf and void all other possible bonds; some might say it was too strong, and being held together by it, facing each other, they truly saw no one and nothing else. But they were good hunters, good debaters, good storytellers; in fact, in all things they were just better. They were beautiful and haughty, and others respected their skills and beauty and also distrusted them secretly, because of the blindness of their bond. But sirens have a respect for things that are, and always put the being of a thing before the questioning of it. There must be a reason for all things, even if the reason will bring pain upon all of us. Us trying to rise above the reason to salvage our comfort would make things worse than bearing the pain. This is how sirens think. So Rea and Pon existed among their group, within it and outside, seemingly above, like a storm hanging above that waits to open up and happen, like a catastrophe already unfolding, but beyond the wills of those who would seek to avoid catastrophe. And all the while others secretly distrusted them, they also secretly adored them. They felt something special when eating something that had been killed by Rea or by Pon. When one of the two sought sex from a member or the group, that member felt honoured, like being visited by an alien feeling, and cherished the embrace while also fearing it."

The child, on hearing this part of the story, looked puzzled. Maybe this story would need retelling. The sun was going down, almost touching the horizon; as the colour of its rays grew hotter and wilder, also the power they had to heat grew weaker. Night was becoming more present. He continued:

"One day Rea and Pon went out hunting together, as they often did; mostly sirens hunt in groups of six to ten, but these two hunted together, just the two of them. They went out from the rocks where the community was congregating at the time, and followed the coast to a place they knew where some big and slow fish lived. In fact, that place is the rocky zone right there, at the end of the beach", said the man, and pointed to their left. The child was silent, quite taken by the story.

"They felt hungry. They swam fast, and when they got to the place, they waited, each behind their rock, knowing the big and slow fish would be coming home from the opposite direction to hide among the bigger rocks. As they waited the sea became cold. They waited for a long time, utterly silent and motionless. Little fish came and nibbled at their skin, and inquisitive fish came to bump on them, but they remained motionless. Then, after a long wait, the big fish appeared. It was heavy and slow, grey in tone and placid-looking. It swam slowly and placidly. When Rea pounced on it, expecting it to turn away toward Pon, the fish just stopped swimming. So she grabbed it and started biting the top of its head, to make the bone explode. The fish didn't resist. By the time it died Pon was there too, not even holding the fish, just touching it, seeing that no help was required from him."

"Then, the fish was dead, and they pushed it toward the beach right there, to eat it. But there were hunters there, human hunters, gathered around a fire and cooking fish as the night fell. When they saw the sirens appear with their huge fish, they stared silently, transfixed by their beauty. Sirens are beautiful, and those two were even more beautiful than most; also no one hardly ever gets to see them from up close. So the hunters watched, as Pon held up the big fish, making sounds and gestures of offering. Why was Pon acting like this? Pon was probably disappointed by how the hunt had happened and wanted to do something interesting. The hunters came up to him, intrigued and amazed. He laid the huge grey fish on the beach in front of them, and gestured toward the fire. He wanted them to cook the big fish, and so they did. Rea stayed back a little, fascinated by what was happening. And when the fish was cooked, the hunters brought it back to Pon, and Pon ate of it. And he gave some of it to Rea, who haughtily ate it too. They were breaking a very important taboo by exchanging with humans, and also especially by eating burnt meat. The fish was delicious, and its taste filled them with pleasure, a kind of pleasure they had not felt before; it was deep and burning, red in colour, dry in texture, and it lit them up. But then their eyes rolled back in their skulls and they had to lay down. The hunters had retreated back to their fire. And they slept there, lying on the sand, with the half eaten cooked fish between them."

"When they woke up the sea had retreated, and they had lost their fish tails. Instead they had legs, human legs, as strong and beautiful as their tails had been. So they got up, excited, and started running around, and then they ran into the land, looking at everything delightedly. But after a while running, they felt an ache for the sea, and went back. They wanted to swim again, but they didn't know how to with their new legs. And from a distance they saw their community, lounging on the rocks and swimming and having fun among the waves, but when they looked up to them none recognized them. So the pair became desperate, and cried for a while. And then they threw themselves from the cliffs, back into the sea, and died. And that was the end of the story of Rea and Pon, the two sirens who were as twins. Did you like it?"

But the child has fallen asleep, god knows at what point in the story; the man has moved himself to a solemn and grave state, and feels that his story is very important. But apparently it hasn't been for the benefit of the child. He laughs, and carries his child back into the home, and lays them in bed, and then he stays on a wooden chair in the room for a while, thinking of the child, of the Progressive Fundamentalists, of the sirens and of the pleasures they find inside the sea. He also thinks he is happy that the child couldn't hear the gloomy ending of his story, though he should've seen that coming, in retrospect. Maybe he'll still try to tell the full story at some point. He goes downstairs to make some tea. Things just keep moving.

THE POSSESSION OF DESIRE

Mark Bolsover

—impossible, then, in the end, I s'ppose, to *know* (for sure, … —finally) how much of your desire you (truly) *own*. … (—?).

…

Supratentorial Craniotomy—Surgery for Organic (extra-/post-) Libidinal – Psycho-sexual purge

(—Operation on the upper part of the brain)

Information for patients

© A. Pope/C. Kaufman Centre HS Foundation

First published February 2[---]

INTRODUCTION

The aim of this leaflet is to provide you with information of the uncommon procedure(s) you are about to have. This leaflet will help you to understand what you can expect before and after the operation. This may be a period of anxiety and uncertainty for you. We hope that this leaflet answers some of the questions that you might have that are related to the procedure.

WHAT CAN I EXPECT FROM THE OPERATION?

The aim of surgery on brain tumours is two-fold.

➢ Remove as much of the abnormal area as possible (if possible, in its entirety) with minimal or no damage to surrounding normal structures.

➢ Ascertain the nature of the abnormality by sending some of it to be looked at under the microscope by the Neuropathologist.

CAN YOU REMOVE IT COMPLETELY?

➢ The factors that determine whether an area of abnormality can be completely removed include:

❖ tissue of origin of the abnormality

❖ area of the brain where the abnormality is located

❖ whether there is a clear margin between the abnormal and normal structures.

➢ There may be important structures like the optic nerve (nerve responsible for seeing), nerves for eye movements, hearing, facial movement, swallowing and coughing, or major blood vessels supplying blood to the brain which might be very close to or within the abnormal area making complete removal difficult.

➢ The area of the brain in which the abnormality is present is also important. Certain areas of the brain that are responsible for important and vital functions (e.g. movement of arm/leg/face, understanding and creating speech and language, centres for eye movements, hearing, vision, breathing, blood pressure etc) could prove a challenge to the surgeon to achieve complete removal of the abnormality without compromising function.

➢ At surgery, if the distinction between the normal and abnormal areas is unclear, then as much of the abnormal area as is safely possible will be removed.

WHAT ARE THE RISKS OF THE OPERATION?

Technically, the procedure is a form of brain damage. However, advances in neurosurgery and anaesthesia have made Supratentorial Craniotomy surgery relatively safe, but some risks still remain:

➤ The risk of death is present and is usually very small, but can vary depending on circumstances.

There is a risk of:

➤ paralysis or weakness of arm or leg,

➤ difficulty in speech or language recognition,

➤ double vision,

➤ decreased vision,

➤ impairment of sensation in the face or the body,

➤ difficulty in swallowing,

➤ and impairment of hearing.

WILL I BE ASLEEP DURING THE OPERATION?

The majority of operations for suspected brain tumours take place with you fully asleep during the procedure. If there are any special circumstances, they will be discussed with you before the operation.

WHAT HAPPENS ON THE DAY OF OPERATION?

➤ On the day of surgery, you will need to fast for at least 6 hours (6 hours for solids and milky drinks and 3 hours for water) prior to administration of the anaesthetic.

WHAT HAPPENS IN THE OPERATING ROOM?

➤ After the anaesthetist has put you to sleep, the surgeon will place you on the operating table in the best position for performing the operation.

➢   The exact site and length of the cut on your head will vary depending on the site and extent of the abnormality that will have been already been explained to you.

➢   After the cut has been made, a piece of bone will be removed and the membranes covering the brain opened to expose the brain.

➢   The 'Stealth' Image guidance system will help accurately identify the location and extent of the abnormality at surgery using the special scan that you had prior to the operation.

➢   After the procedure has been performed, the bone piece is put back and secured with tiny plates and the wound sewn back with sutures.

➢   The skin stitches that you will have after surgery will be removed in 5–7 days.

➢   You may have a drain (to drain excess blood and fluid from under the scalp), which will be removed a day or two following surgery.

➢   You will also probably have an intravenous line in your arm, which will be removed when you are ready to eat and drink.

➢   Occasionally, you might have a urinary catheter (inserted in the operating room to help drain the urine from your bladder) when you wake up. This will usually be removed the next day or so when you can get out of bed.

➢   You will be given adequate pain relief after surgery to make you comfortable and specialists from the pain management team will speak to you if there are any particular concerns.

...

(on the eve.
(hotel).
...)

quiet. …

…

tomorrow morning.

(*hhuh-(…) – v-ph-(w)eewh. …*).

tomorrow morning. tomorrow morning.

tomorrow morning.

…

(—alone.) …

(near) silence.

light. … —is that, *strange,*… —muted (dusty?), slightly airless, muffled light (dinge), … —from (of) (sun's)light, *wan*(-thin)-pale (gentle-frail) white.

… —*stunted* (yes),—by that thick, (yet) slight… translucent of (institutional) cream-yellow-ochre hotel (window) curtains. …
(room dull).

warm.

(c'n tell it's light out. (still). …).

… —bed's… *cool. and firm.* (fresh made).
(under me).

hotel.

room.
(… —bland cream-white-*beige* ('v all places like)…).

—*waiting*.
(now).

…

and tomorrow (*now*), …

—I —**go under.** …

(at the centre. …).

...

 … **—Supratentorial Craniotomy—Surgery for Organic (extra-/post-) Libidinal – Psycho-sexual purge**
 (Operation on the upper part of the brain)
(… —*"Information.—for patients"*. …).

—the operation.
(surgical.—procedure. …).
(operating *theatric*. …)

(*anaesthesia*).

(—an incision (cut). ...
(—*open*.

—the cranium. ...)

...and.—*purge*. (t' *expunge*)—(all 'v) the structures *(shape)*-... the *matter*...
—'v desire (—libidinal.—psycho-sex)...

—over ('long)... —the *surface* of my brain. ...).

...

(i). on the reformation of the conscience.
(on *doubt*—& (toward) the *undoing* of shame (regret)). ...

—*how much,* (if, indeed, any) of "my" desire do I actually **own**. ...
—?

(... —how much am I prepared to *admit* that I own. ... —? ...).

(—how much (—*to what extent*. ...) am I, in fact, possessed *by* desire.
(—(by) the desire that is—that was (has never been)—truly *mine* (my
own-to own). ... —?).

...

... —*against which* (cold) reason—*struggles*. ...

(… —don't **trust** the (image of—) the… *"lust"* for—"woman"(-"women")—the other—, … or the way(-ways) in which I *(feel* I*)* desire. …

… —what has been **made**, then, of sexual desire (—its (supposéd) (pre-)dominance (… —*amplification (*seeming)) in-for "men"… —its legitimisation, centralisation, and (apparent) inescapability. (—*atavistic*(?)—inherited. …). …).

(—attempts to *resist.* … —to comprehend, and to compensate for.

—to **control**. …).

…

if the subject

…

(…

if.

…

(…) —if the subject
(—the I that *says* "I" …

—that *is*—*by* (-in-through) saying "I")…

… —the "I" saying *"I,"*—now, as I think this (-these thoughts). …).

is *formed* …

—in a moment of recognition. ...

—the *specular image* ...
(—the moment of (first)... —*looking in a(-the)* **mirror**. ...

... —seeing there the reflected image (... —the image 'v the *body*—whole-*complete*
(... —bounded round (apparent) by-at the edges(-margins) (—'v the (body's) *frame* (—framed)). ...

(... —(apparently) **discrete,** ... and... —*realised.* ...).

... a—*false,* (-a **mis-)** *recognition,* then, ... —of (-with-*as*) the unified (self-identical) (specular-mirror) image. ...).

and/or...

—*thrust.*—in-to (into) language... —*the chain of signification.* ...
(—formed by language... —(pre-existing-extant) values-prejudices. ...).

—in-through-by (the act 'v) naming (—by being **named.**)
(... —the *projection* (upon,—fr'm without) of an *ideal.* ... —the *this-ness,*—in the name,—of what "I" am-*ought* to be (—the *ideal...* —*held-placed above-before* me. ...).
(—*to be aimed (always)* **toward. ...**

—toward the(-that) (false.-illusion-delusional) (specular) image (
... —seemingly self-identical, complete(-whole)—**realised.** ...
(saturated-... —*comprised,* by-of values-prejudices (prejudicial)... —inherited (—from without) (—thrust upon). ...).

...

—a *projection.* (projected).

...

—an **imposition.** (*yes*).
(—to only ever be aimed **toward.** ...).

...

... —cannot-could not ever (truly)... —*gain identity* with the *ideal-image.*

...

... —the image which makes me (—(makes) the subject. ... —*the I that says "I"* ...) possible (at all).
(... —which *appears* (, then,) to be... —the *condition* of my possibility (—**transcendental** (a priori), ...
(made.(-forged).—in the yearning for identity with (-to attain). ...).

and yet. ...

...

and yet, which, (always, and at the *same time)* is impossible (... — impossible to gain-attain identity with(-to)),

and, thus, is (—always, ... and at the *same time...*), then, ... —the condition of (my) *im*-possibility...
(... —that which (appears to) make me (possible), ... and yet which makes me (, finally,) *impossible.* ...).

—an *ideal*(-the image)… forever (inexorably(-ineluct)… —***alien***. …
(… —forever ***alienated*** (from). …).

then, …

…

… —formed by, … —and never (truly) in *possession of* (…)— …*values* (
… —prejudices-conditions

—of which I'm not—and could never be—*conscious.* …)

(—always already *possessed **by***. …).

(… —desire. … already (always) conditioned—from without. …

(and) … —*always desire to desire in the way **I ought** to desire.*
(never my own).

…).

…

… —how much dictated (to-by—in the *thrall* of) memory(-memories)—
(adolescent) embarrass (wounded pride—the self-opinion *(would)*),—
guilt-***shame***. …

—? …

(how desperate …)

and her pure (—a **crystal**) blue eyes... —shone... —shone with sarcasm when she was tearing me apart (—*laughing, a shrewd, complicit, intelligent smile.*

...

to know and to trust not to be hurt and not to hurt in those (sharp, barbed) exchanges...).

her face.—*so beautiful.* her long, full dark hair (—*curls-waves slight*). her soft small sharp mouth. her soft pale skin,—milky, warm and creamy (*bitter-sweet (slight) to the taste,—soft and smooth to (the) touch...*)...

...

—how *desperate* I was—to make love to her...
((—o-ahh—**God.**)...

—*need to* **hold** *(—tight-close)...kissing (hungry. desperate...).—soft* **(yielding,** *smooth)* **warm** *of skin (on skin) (flesh). ... —the yield* **(give)** *as move inside (warm) (—so soft (velvet) and yet holds so tight...)—***need.** **(intense** *(sharp?) aching)—to* **thrust...** *(that—***tension (hunger)—***in-between us...* **heat.**—*that needs us to fuck (to* **consummate***)...).*

and *ache.—***desperate...**
(—that... **ache.** *... —(feel I)* **need** *it to get* **worse***...).*
  (—a hot, yearning, ache
    in the pit of the chest
        felt...)

(... —drawn out. distended—
membrane-thin (at the outer
boundary).—a hollow, electric
feeling-sensed. (taut). ...

—in need of substance. (—a
void.—a lack.).—strange. ...
—emerges from being over-
full...)

aches
(—aay-k(hu)sss. ...).

—how... *unworthy-**low*** (—***afraid***), though, I *(still)* feel myself...
(—*social inadequate.*—**emotional...** *(—awkwardness.*—**anxiety...**)...
—*afraid of women—sex (embarrassment*—**rejection**)... *(—need to be loved-
accepted)...*).

...

all those times.
(knowing better).

... —all those times. ... —(all those times) that I (have. ever.)... *reduced* (—*friends* ('v mine), even ...) to their bodies – their *looks*-"sex(ual) appeal". ...

... —out of... *awkwardness* (shyness, discomfort,—*fear*... —'v women, fear 'v sex,—fear 'v *rejection*. ...), ... out of *drunkenness*, out 'v *frustration* (... with other things, ... —myself,—a situation(-circumstance), ... boredom, embarrassment, ...), ... —out 'v(-fr'm) an *inarticulate*, (vague-unfocussed,—reluctant), *impotent,* (...—a) *poorly sublimated—anger*. ...
(frustration, boredom, embarrassment(-humiliat), ...

—a dull, pervasive, *pulsing* (puls) (tight, hollow, hard-'lectric—*inhibited* (feels) (—(a) **pushing out** ('gainst the edges-th' limits 'v), and in(-through-out fr'm) the *centre-chest*. ...

—unwelcome, and distasteful (repuls), yet obstinat, strong (urgent), and (, sadly,) *compelling*. (... —urged-impulsed. to act against (-over-ouwith) *reason)*, ... and, out of a childish(-adolesc), self-indulgent, (partial-)self-destructive (so to) inability (felt) to (want to) *resist* (—*a need* (felt) to be *helped,* ... —for *intimacy* (in-of some-of any sort-form that can be accomplished), ... —for (a) **relief,** ...

... **—lash out.**
(with an already *bad – conscience*. ...).

...

—*in spite of myself.—?* ...
(—despite *knowing better*. ...).

...

—in(de)spite of an *awareness.* of how… wrong, … —(how) unfair, and reductive, and demeaning.
(—how uncomfortable (discomfiting), (and) how unsettling. …).

… —out 'v a ***failure***—to acknowledge-address that-those behaviour(s) (prejudish)—of (what it is to be) *male* (—performing the status 'v) (and to relate to others). …
(… —(out of) an inexcusable *lack* 'v (full) awareness-comprehens. of (the)… ***diminishment.*** (yes). …

… —the diminishment 'v women(-others), but, *as much* ('n' at th' same),—of myself. .
(… —a *lack.* of self-scrutiny, (of self-contempt), … —of self-control (self-*mastery)*—(of) ***autonomy*** (fr'm) (—self-*defining* (-self-determine)).

…

—that that which poses(-is *presented)* as—***power*** (… —as *active,*—as *agency)* (… —the *sub-ordination* 'v others, … —the reduction to sex)… is, in (—as a matter 'v—)fact, … —a form of ***re-****active* weak (cowardly-craven) *acquiescence* (uncritical), to a form-values, … —*projected* upon-on(-to—onto), … —fr'm *without.* …

((in fact), … —a *lack.*—of **freedom.**(-self-create)). …).

(… and. … —I don't want to be a coward… —t' be *subject(ed)* to.

(shame. (regret)). …).

on the corruption of tenderness. …

(—?). ...

she

... —wrote (and *published)* a... "novelette"... —(in which) casting-she cast me(—?) as a lonely, bureaucratic (unimaginative—*pe-dant)* (—freelance writer-administrator), desperate, and deluded fantasist. ...

—(as) a **stalker**. ...
(—?)

(*hmm*).

...

... —what. (...)

—is there a... —(definite) *point*... (or)(a)—*line*, ... beyond which... *tenderness*... flips-folds (over), ... and becomes (turns (over) into) something... *unwholesome*. ... —"creepy," and... —*disturbing*. ...

—?

•••

— ... a line, (then),—between... —*adoration* (?)... —*devotion* (so to.—sic), and simple, unhealthy (—morbid) *obsession*. ... (—? ...).

...

—where tenderness is *turned*, ... —in-by its own *impotence* (—a failure.—t' ever have *connected* with its object(-focus).)—then, (perhaps)

(—into its *opposite*. ...). ...

... —?

The Devil's Lamp. ...

—article (—a title.-headline. ...) seen (I saw). (in-through passing).
(—a news-paper... -maga-zine. ...).

...

... —

"I ALWAYS DUMP MY GIRLFRIENDS AFTER 18 MONTHS. WHAT AM I SO AFRAID OF?" ...

(... —'*always*'. ... '*afraid*'. ... '*I/my*'. ... ...).

...

... —***aware***. 'v the... *smallness(yes)*-idiocy, ... —th'... self-sabotage
(so to), ...

—the lack 'v dignity... —lack of ***shame***. ...
(... —ashamed *(should)*, 'v the *lowness*, and of *advertising* ('v same)), in-'v
their behaviour. ...

and, *but yet*, ... —t' *indulge* (self) in it, anyway. (—persist(s): '*always*,' 'I/
my' ...).

…

—makes me think(-reminds),… 'v that painting. … —by Francisco de Goya. …

… —(a) priest.—in robes (enrobed). … —*leans in* (—'gainst-b'fore a backdrop-ground, dark-shadowed. …
(… —those strange-uncanny (demonic?) horse-men.—stalk-cavort. …). …

… —pouring oil—into the Devil's (—goat-horned-skulled. Breasted) Lamp (—'llumines (hot-bright, dusty (light)—(a) *pool* 'v light. …). …

… **—*horrified*** (… —hand over mouth. … —eyes (wide)—*stare,* in moral-mortal terror-(seeming… *righteous) disgust…*) that the Devil should be fuelled. …

…

**(—in(-of) the—half-waking(-woken) state. …
(in which)—the past resolutely refuses to *fuck off*. …).**

—in a tweet. …

—a line. (apocryphally?) attributed to Nietzsche. …

—*'When we are tired, we are attacked by ideas we conquered long ago.'*

…

yes.

—. —IN(-OF) THE—HALF-WAKING(-WOKEN) STATE. ...

... —a... *letting down* (so to.—sic) of the (conscious) *guard(s)*-... barriers.
...

... —a **regression.** (yes). ...

—back. (down).—in-to (into) **habit...** —habits, (otherwise), once
overcome. ...
(ingrained,—habituated responses *(involunt).* ...

—tics. ...).
(modes, 'n' shapes of thought(-the mind). ...).

...

... —(a question 'v)—*teasing*(-tease) *apart* (feels—*must* ...).—the...
layers-strata(?)—the... *structure* (rather)—(in-'v the mind).

—of (in-'v) *desire.*

(—in a(-in any) *given moment.* ...).

...

(ii). the reversal of sex.
(—(to) **get out.** ... —*from under it.* ...).

—I want (... —*desire.* (ironic)), then, ...

—to purge-(to) *expunge,* ...

—in order to discover...

—how much of my desire do I (truly) *own.* ... —?

(—(the question of) **what is left,**—when(once) all (the) outer values-influences (-prejudices) have been *expunged.* ...

—? ...).

...

(... —there's no **need** for any*(all)* 'v this... dross (moments), that-which... **percolates** (*(yes).* ... —*up),* ... —from *(down)* the (seeming) hidden (—dull-dark (deep) brown-(slate-dark) grey shadow(ed) gloom (warm,—*dusty)* seeming) *depths* (in-)'v memory(ies) (emerge).

(... —always... *there (—present,* still, somehow), ... —but... —*unaware* ('v) there

(... —*gaps* (lacoon)). ...

—absent-*non-exist,* until *re-called* (... awakened-*ac-tiv-ated* (called—again... —(a) (re-)*summons*(ed)). ...)
(... —all ('v) the *details,* still). ...).

(... —no **use** (... t' me). ... —'v no *value*(worth). (... —*no* **purpose,** but to *hang,* always, (there, still,) ... —as a *weight*(-weights) (—'nnecessary burden)... (... and wait(s). ... —t' *resurface.* (recalled). (out). ...

and *t' bother* (—humiliat) the conscience. *(shame.* regret). ...).

...

—the aesthetic, and (... —*reduced to.* ...)—the libidinal-commercial.
...

(—?).

... —

(—the... —*fascination* (entrancing (-fixate)), of(-in-with) **beauty**. ...
(hmm). ...).

(the-a)... **aesthetic reality** (sic. so to. ...). ...
(—the *objective* (abstract-*disinterested* (—without *interest))-observable* fact
(sic)...

—of (the) *beauty.*

—*confused.* in-with (—**reduced** to (exclusive)). ...

(with)—*desire.* ...   (—to *touch*(-caress)).
(—excitation. (lust?)).

libidinal(childish)-*commercial.*   ...   (emotional-sexual—*economic*
ownership).—?

(... *how much* (if any) in-of that desire (so to) is **genuine** (—?)... —
genuinely *mine* (—*comes from me...* —organically (so to.—sic),...
—'naturally'-inevitably...), and not... —encoded. ... —a cultural
(en-cultured (social-societ) construct-phenom. ... —? ...).

...

—(always)(?)—a desire to **possess.** (?— ... —to **consume.** ... —?).
(—t' have possession (possessed) of the beauty (—*access* to (excluse)),
in-'v—seen (, then), as *object*-stimulus... **—thing** *(only).*
(... —no recognition.—of *autonomous*... —intellectual(psych), ...
emotional, ... political,—person(-hood) – **agency.**
(—discounted. ...).

(and, therefore,

(always also)...)

—no **empathy.**
(... —is it *no* empathy—an absolute state (—an... *incapacity*
(-incapability)), ... or. Is-has empathy been... —overcome (so to) (—
overwhelmed. ...)... —suspended-*shut off.* ... —? ...).

...

is desire (—the *limits* of, as felt-experienced—at this point-juncture of
time-history (socio-politic) *genuine,* ... or, is the need (felt) to possess-t'
have possessed (consume – consumed) entirely encoded-ingrained
(-acquired-(re-)enforced)... —a *prejudice* (inherited). ... —?

...

—a *mis-apprehension.* ... —an assumption. ... —that all relationships-to
(-of coming-into-contact(s)-with) must—by their 'nature' (supposed)—
be *sexual* in 'nature'. ... (—?).
(—NAY–CHA. ...).

—and... —cuts in (—(a) **habit**)-habitual) (so to), ... —before any and all other (possible) relationships-to (—perspectives, &c. ...)-considerations, can (—are given time-the chance-opportunity to) form(—considered). ...

—the libidinal(-commercial)-*sexual,* ... —placed fore-uppermost, (and given-granted, thus-then, ... —***priority***.
(—here, in the senses (both) of *temporal* priority, though, also, (by ways 'n' means), at the same time, (an) *ontological* priority, ... but also (an) *impulsion (—urgent.* (physical-biologic.—*NAY–CHA.* ...))

—a consummation *devoutly* t' be ...).

from when it will have been revealed.

...

—a *point.* ...

—(from) on Hegel's *(Phenom.enology),* ... —(and) the 'Master/Slave' (—dialectic).

...

... —(when it will have been revealed) that the 'slave,' in fact, contains-possesses the **freedom** that would *appear* to be the (sole) province-domain-prerogative of the 'Master'...

(… freedom. … —as *labour* on, and (therefore) *access to,* the world, … in fact (precisely) denied in-to the 'Master,'—who is revealed (thus) in their dependence-the dependent state-*term*-consciousness, …

—in absolute reliance (dependent), upon the work of the 'slave,'—*upon their behalf*—… on-in the world. …). …

—'slavery,' thus, can *only* be maintained through the practice-exercise of (a) violence(-coercion), and oppression, … —(that is) *artificially,* and borrowed (acquired) from without (from outwith the (supposéd) 'Master' term)
(—from some other,—*higher,* agency (—state, &c. …). …

—fundamentally **hypocritical** (and cowardly) in **denial**-ignorance (forced-)suppression of the structure-(internal, ineluctable) logic. … (—*dishonesty*).

—women *reduced* to secondary-minor, *possessed*-consumed term, … — only through the imposition of oppression (and oppressive violence),— ignorance-suppression of the (ineluctable) logic of labour-*freedom.*

… —mistaken prejudice. …

—that that *(false)* priority must be indulged-satisfied. (… —that it is *'natural'* (-inevitable-ineluctable) to want-to *need(?)* this to be the case. …).

—at the cost of all else (possible).

(… —that *not to* do so… —to strive to indulge, and to possess (solely sexually—verbal-physical …), is—personal, 'masculine' (man)— **failure** (absolute). …

—the (inevitable) element-moment-quantum of *anxiety in-'v desire* (at least in this form,—here. …).

…

—that there is a *necessity,* and a (corresponding) *entitlement* to indulge.
…
(… —must be allowed to. (—not prevented. by opposing, autonomous will-agency *(freedom)*. …

and, if not, … that positions of power-influence can-may be *abused* to enable to indulge. …

—as… *compensation.*—for an-the otherwise impotent(ce).
(—both as sexual, and (yet) also as existential—*agency.* …).

…

… —desire.—*not genuine.* … —?

… —(a) *confusion*—of the aesthetic (objective) (so to—sic), and-with *necessity* of-to sexual (libidinal-commercial) interpretation of-response to, and sexual (excluse) desire.
(—to desire,—*automatically,* primarily, (exclusively?). sexually-libidinally-commercially (—ownership-possession-consumption) …).

—that that is *right,* and true, and *'natural'* (inevitable).
(and that this *must* find satiation-satisfact (—an *entitlement.* … —a *'right'.* …).).

…

—cuts off. from the recognition—of autonomy-*freedom.* ... —of friendship. ...
(—*opposed,* then, in fact, ...

—to the-that *attraction* (mutual) that grows (mutual)—from conversation-talking, getting to know, wit, warmth, ... &c. ...

—c'n see as *friend,* or (business, personal, &c.) *associate,* and have an *appreciation* of the aesthetic (remain), with no necessit-impetus, and no verbal-physical (harassment-assault-abuse)...).

...

the *tendrils* (—the structure-networks of desire), ... &—the leap. ...

...

... —the structure (... —*network*(s)) 'v desire. ...

...

... —in... tendrils (*veined.*—in *strands.* ...) (... —*black* (dark) (*oil* (crude))—in sheen (shine-*glistens*) viscous. out. (radial-ate).

... —(over-)'cross the *mind.* (in radials. out). ... (—*see* ...).

(—'cross the... *surface* (-the *tissue* (matter) 'v the brain's surface ((face)). ...)

...

—to *expunge*. ...

the *leap*. ...

...

and time, ... —*falls*. ... —*slots* (... —*settles*. fits).—back down (—the *shape* 'v ...).

... —a... *tension* (anxiety) (dramat). ...

—*released*. (... —exhausted in-by being *realised)*.
(—*purged*.

—*incorporated*, and (, now,) *accepted*. ...).

—(and) a *moment* (, then,) quiet(-still), ... —of *calm*. (it is accomplished).
...).

then, before (, then,) ...

—the *opening*,—of a gateway, ... —t' the *next moment* (—in-'v crisis). ...

...

—the *release*. (out). (—free-liberat, f'r a *moment)*. ...

... —the-an... *aura* (transluce), 'v blue light. ... —surrounds(-envelopes). ...

... —begins in-'t the *heart* (in) (-the centre-chest) (felt).
(nervs-tense(d) (hard). ... a—*cool,* (... a) hollow aching in-'v. ...).

—a sudden... **burst**(-a *pulse*).—*electric*
(... —a *crack* (electro-static)—burst ('v lightning) (*augenblick*). crackles
– *screams* (liquid).**-sings.** ... (crescendo).

—a hissing-deep sighing rush (in *waves)*. ...).

—*tears* the heart (apart.—in two-ain) (felt).
(... —an... anxiet **quaking** (tight, sharp, 'lectric *thrill)*—in the gut's
pit(-pelvic)... —vertiginous. ...
(—a *lift* (—a rise.—lifting) (felt). ...).

(... —*pushes.* out. ...

—sharp, hot ache.—tears.—(at) the boundaries-th' limits 'v. ...).

...

—two flashes (forking (forks)-ribbons)—'v lightning (bolts) electric. ...

—*pass* (up. 'n' down ...)—*through* the body. (tensing.—in waves (—*rise.*
and *fall.* ...)).

(cool nerv tense, and expand (with)...).

—lacerates. ... (—*laceration*).

and. ... *—return. (—rejoin).*

to meet.

and *collapse.* (—back in(ward)to). ...

and... *—explode.* (*—over-charged*).—out.—in   waves...   *—rays*
(beam)—radial. ...

... *—too much* energy (-a surfeit) (will)—in-'v the heart-chest (felt).

—explode out. ...

—in a burst (*—a flash),* 'v pure, blinding *blue light* (electric).

...

—the *leap.*
(, then, ... —in-through time. (out. *up* (and rising). ...).

—sublime.

... *—the creation of (a form of)...* *—artificial intelligence.*
(—in a way. ...).

...

REMEMBER THAT YOU'VE FORGOTTEN. ...

...

(... *—a selective editing.* ...).

(and) to lay the (physiological-psychological) foundations for *new* *b*ehaviours and experiential modes. (so to.—sic? ...). ...

—liberated from *inherited* patterns*(-habits),* ... —prejudices, of perceiving, reacting, and behaving.

... —a... *bid,* ... —for (—genuine... -thoroughgoing) (intellectual) ***freedom.*** ...

—to, truly, *own* (—to *master*(-t' have mastery *over)* desire.

...

—the possession, *then, of desire.* ...

...

(...) —to... —*expunge habit(s)* (yes), and memory(-ies). ...
(as if each... —a *fragment* (in-on-of the mind. (—the *brain* (organ)—?
...).

...

but, ... —no.

because, how, then, could(-would) you (be able to) feel the benefit. ...
—?

... —you would have to remember that you had forgotten, and (the nature of) what it was that you had forgotten (—and, therefore(-thus), ... why it was you *willed* its forgetting. ...).

...

... —Dante (Aligheri)'s *Purgatory* (—*Il Purgatorio*). ... —the second '*Cantica*' of *The Comedy [Divine]*. ...

...

—the (river) *Lethe*
(... —in the midst of the *Earthly Paradise,* in-on *Mount Purgatory,* for Dante, then, (Dantean Cosmology)... (and)— not (in-'v) the *underworld(-**Hell**)*, (as it was in-f'r *ol' Plato)*...).

...

Into the stream she'd drawn me in my faint,
Throat-high, and now, towing me after her,
Light as a shuttle o'er the water went.

"*Asperges me*" [—"*thou shalt **purge** me*"] I heard, as I drew near
The blissful brink, so sweetly as to drown
Power to recall, far more to write it here.

She stretched both hands, she seized me by the crown,
Did that fair lady, and she plunged me in,
So that I needs must drink the water down;

Then drew me forth and led me, washed and clean [...]

(... —Dorothy L. Sayers' translation. ...

—(in-fr'm) 'CANTO XXXI,'—315-321, ll.94-103 (317-318). ...).

and ...

(—then).

... —the *Eunoë.*

...

Here I protested: "But I can't recall
That I ever estranged myself from you:
For that, my conscience feels no twinge at all."

"And if thou hast forgotten it – go to,
Remember" – she was smiling as she spoke –
"Thou'st drunk to-day of Lethe: yea, and true

It is, if fire may be inferred from smoke,
From this oblivion we may well adduce
Proof of thy guilt – false will and fealty broke.

[...]

Look, flowing yonder, there is Eunoë;
Conduct him there, and in it, as thy use is,

Restore his fainting powers' vitality."

[...]

From those most holy waters, born anew
I came, like trees by change of calendars
Renewed with new-sprung foliage through and through,

Pure and prepared to leap up to the stars.
(... —(in-fr'm) 'CANTO XXXIII,' 331-339, ll.91-145 (333-335).
...).

...

—forgetting *and* recollection (—*without guilt*), in-of the rivers *Lethe* and *Eunoe,* (respect).

...

instead, (then), ...

—the expunging(-purgation) of memory (—habit-prejudice), ... (*and,* then,) with the *restoration* (of the memory of),—without (the same) *affect(s).* ...
(... —remembering what it was to have desired in that way(-those ways), ... —without (still) being a subject to. ... (—t' remember-retain what am, now (—*then.* (—will be ...)) *free from.* ...).

...

(... —the question is... —*must always* **be**— ... ...

—not (to be) *free* ***from*** what (... —the past, ... prejudices (-habit(s) (bad-)), ... —lust, humiliat, (&c.). ...), but, ... —*free* ***for*** *what* (... — *to(-**toward***) what (the future (yet)). ... —? ...).

...

(... —yes. ...

—free from the *burden* (felt-thought), ... —'v the past,—'v prejudice and *wrong behaviour,* humiliation, (&c. and so. ...), ... but in order, *then,* to... *accomplish* what (... —in that, brave, new, *state* of freedom. ...) ... —?
(... —*without(outwith)* the burden... ... —what it *provides* (as constant, *repulsive* stimulus (so to)... —*to never be that again.* ... —what would be left to achieve... —?

(and would I even be *capable*... —?).

...).

...

and... (...)

—look forward, in hopes, to looking forward in hopes.

THE CAUSEWAY
Matthew Crowley

There's nothing here.

Only silence. So complete it finds resonance, so absolute it rings. A continuous wavering note, all empty lines and phrases, all full of potential, all latent. I hear my heart. Its beating, and I'm naked, and I'm sodden and exposed. Arms hang loose at my sides. Erratic drip tracks run their length. Timid and slow. Uniting and gathering pace, at unexpected intervals, matting fine hairs in undular patterns, prickling the skin as they run. Skinless gourds gather at my fingertips, where they hang in anticipation until, unable to bear their own weight, they drop to the floor. There's a syncopated plip, plip-plip, plip; pock--pock- -pock, as they acne the mud at my feet. I call out. A dry squawk I try to re-swallow. I search for a violence in my voice. The silence smothers everything. I'm nothing here. But I am here.

. . .

My breath finds a hold in the silence. My imagination occupies the nothing with passive imperial dreams. I have arrived. I am here. I am come. It comes heavy measured, the breath. Chest rising repeatedly against my uniform, steady, in, and out, in, and out, in, and out. The exhalations caught in the upturned collar of my greatcoat. Contained there, momentarily, in the certainty of its wool-muffled acoustic. My breath's amplified as I glance at the kitbag that makes a blunt point against my shoulder. Close shorn hairs catch the collar's rough nap as I turn into it. Errant strands have escaped the warp. Translucent when caught alone in the light. Breathe. I ache, dull and uncomplicated, with hard work. A rifle dangles at my other side. It clacks against me as I reach inside the collar and knead the base of my neck. My hands are rough callous hands. Fingers swollen with strength and over-use. Each nail flat and filthy-black. Skin worn tight. Ground dirt stains lines that intersect it. My shirt's cuff brushes my ear, soft and smooth, but starched stiff. I'm in dress uniform, tired from marching, but not in fatigues. I look down at the mirror-shine elevens beneath knife-edge creases. The movement exposes my neck. A breath of nothing seeps in over the collar, sterile and scentless. I shiver, a subtle convulsion, and hunker down tight into the neatness of myself. Then, secure in darts and creases, I turn to face the wind.

A wooden causeway ekes out over shallow water. Unbending, but ever-depleting, it stretches farther back than I can see. The sleepers of a thin-gauge rail scud the beams as it stretches for the horizon. The water it crosses refuses to ripple, even as the wind takes up, reluctant to spoil the silence with its lapping. A small handcar sits squat a few metres from where I stand. It must be how I arrived, but its wheels are rusted thick. It rocks gently, side-to-side on its trucks, as the wind gains strength. Lolling. A motionless gait that throws out faint whines whenever the axles find their bearings. Each gust presses my trousers flat against my shins. Forces me to squint my eyes. I turn my back, hunch my shoulders, and lift my collar up over my ears. The wind is temporarily drowned by the sound of my breath contained. Increasing its efforts to be heard it tugs violently my clothes, flagging the fronts of my trousers, sharpening their creases and snapping their edges against nothing while the sleepers run under me. They dissect my path as they dash on into the meadow. Their thick black shapes punctuate the field. The measure between them erratic as some are absent from their posts. The smell of them, their thick-sweet-tar, is wed to the wet ground as it tacks up through the thin cold air. Long grass swallows the last of them as the rail peters out. The grass does what the water daren't. Adopting its movement in the wind. Great inverted waves ebb and flow as their stems bow in succession. Each whispering against the next, a thousand whispers, more, many more, producing a muted roar that mimics the water's absent gush.

A memory of the sea. Which sea? Where? And when? The shingle wheeled up the beach with a lulling shush. The waves quietened us. I held your hand. Your hand was soft in mine. My soft hands. I whispered to you. We laughed. The beach was empty, but for us. Or maybe it just seemed that way.

The wind blows the memory clear. Urging me on. Pushing me forward. Lifting the kitbag from my shoulder. Leaving me unbalanced. Head down, shoulders hunched, I move. Measured steps toward the outpost. The ground holds fast where roots are strong. Small clear pools well up around my shoes. They brim at the edge of the sole, as the saturated earth takes my weight. Pendulous, the kitbag swings at my side, thumping against me with each alternate step. Its exhausting heft a comfort on the root sprung grass. Sparse clouds shift rapid across the low-hung sky. Puddles bounce the clouds back as they graze above me. I march on. The grass has lost numbers further in the field. Its networks of roots are weakened. There, the ground gives but doesn't give back. Shallow mud generously welcomes each step, but then refuses to release my shoe. Slaked vacuums that make each new step harder than the last. The grass churns about me. Fresh meadow riptides. Hiding a ground that wants to swallow me whole. I march on. Kitbag thumping alternate step. Rifle keeping time on the other shoulder. I march on. Currents of wind run toward the outpost. The bunker door gulps it in as it sits waiting for me. Drinking and drowning. I march on. Toward the door. I march on. Two small round windows, the outpost's myopic eyes, squint back at me across the field. They blink as they catch the light. My breath is caught in my collar. I feel its moisture between my cheek and the wool. I march on. The kitbag's canvas rasps along my side. Its mass thuds through me. With me, against me, with every other step. Everything clear and muffled and contained. My chest rises and falls, rises and falls, rises, and falls, rises, and falls; working to move the weight I carry.

The wind frequently changes, pace, direction, strength; briefly, uncertain, but stubborn, and always moving. The door of the outpost sucks it in. Gross-rusted, it gulps it in screeching and clangs shut. Gulps it in screeching and clangs shut. Gulps it in screeching and clangs shut. Huge noises made small in the expanse of the air. I raise my head to judge the distance, leaving my feet unattended. The breath escapes my collar. I see it rise before me, great clouds of it dispersing, like drops of white ink in water. Between clangs the wind drops. The door creaks ajar again. A lower sound. Slow and apologetic. Mournful. A dirge of sticky hinges. Hinges that quickly screech cruelly again. The door caught creeping open. The wind interrupting with another violent clang. Creak-screech-clang. Creak-screech-clang. Creak-screech-clang. The mechanics of a strange laugh. I march on. The outpost laughing. At me or with me. I march on. To the gulping laughing door. To the threshold. I march on. To the cause that brought me here. To my post. To an order. I think. After. This is it.

I don't remember arriving at the cause, or what brought me to it. It must have been early in winter though, because the leaves had all fallen but weren't rotten under foot. The bareness of the trees revealed their wounds. I remember the splintered bark where the poc-poc- poc…poc-poc-poc-poc of machine guns had scarred them. I remember the defiance evident in every gnarled branch. A stubborn deciduous honesty. I don't remember who sent me here. Only the order itself. And the wider order; the general order.

The outpost is well sheltered. The cause the only way in, or out. The billet is a bunker. A simple thing, gaping and laughing and blinking its myopic eyes. One room, two parts. The front a low-rise concrete pill-box, the back dug-out of the cliff that rises up, sheer and menacing, behind it. I took stock on arrival. Stood still, on the threshold.

Holding the door mid-cackle. The bunker smelled of memories. It smelled of an irretrievable past. It smelled of the twentieth century; of mould and dust and engine grease; stale beer and sour wine; leather, metal, tobacco; of seasoned wood, sweat-varnished through use; and damp concrete and shit and vomit and blood, that unmistakable iron-copper-tang. The room itself was largely empty. A small Formica topped table, with one leg shorter than the others, stood uncertainly to the left of the door. It would groan pleadingly as it rocked when in use. A vinyl cushioned chair sat next to it, but didn't match, and always looked lonely. The table was comfortable despite its handicap. Even tables with one short leg are used to standing on their own. Chairs need company.

Two reinforced porthole windows cast pillars of sun down into the room. Disturbed dust froths, made to dance by their downcast beams. I learned to watch two plates of sun as they slowly phased across the room. I'd wait for definite circles to form and fade. Perfectly round at noon. Ellipsed by the uncertainty of the afternoon. I appreciated the theatre of their synchronous dance. There was a time each day when the spotlight fell upon the chair. It emphasised its loneliness and, occasionally, reminded me of mine. But, I would think, it's only dust and light and furniture, and I would think no more of it, until I thought of it again. Thinking is no cure for loneliness, but it's reliable company in solitude.

I remember stories I made up to entertain you. Not lies, not really, things that could have happened, but didn't. The lamppost I walked into. The inappropriate outfit I wore to an important event. The rude shop keeper I put back in place. The cubicle lock that broke in my hand. The gum I sat in. The wedding I'd stumbled into. Or was it a wake? The slapstick of everyday. Little gems of it I'd polished just for you, just enough to see you smile, to bring out the frill of your laugh and that little shake of your head. Inventions that were more real than ever to me now. Remembering each tale as if it had happened. Each memory, which is what they'd become, jostled for position as if competing to be the one that pretended to have happened that day. But, in their immediacy, they were all further out of reach. Further removed from a truth that I still understood. More unbelievable, more farfetched, more implausible. That everyday was gone.

A small loose-jointed dresser stands drunk against the far left wall. Its shelves run away to the back of the room as you look at them. They're empty. But for a leather framed photograph of a young private in uniform. The angle of the shelf inclines his head, making him inquisitive. He peers into the room questioningly. His clean young face persistently asking you why you're here. Throwing accusations that deflect your own queries. He offers no explanations for his presence. In front of the picture is a gold wedding band. It winks through the dust, asking to be picked up. It wants to be held. In time I came to believe they were offerings, the photo and the ring, that they'd been left there to appease some ill-tempered spirit, to break a curse, or bind a spell. Perhaps they'd been given to the cause so that the private could simply slip away. When I thought of his departure his gaze became unbearable. The barb of a patronising glint developed. It pierces you and holds you fast. It hooks and draws you in. Still, I never touch the private or his gold. He stays in his place. I stay in mine.

Facing the dresser is a cot bed. It sits tight to the opposite wall. Metal frame, heather-stuffed calico mattress, low-slung across canvas webbing straps. The anonymous private's glare falls directly on it. I feel him watching me as I try to sleep. Wondering how long I will last. The bed's soft, it welcomes a body warmly, but I can find no comfort in it. The sheets never feel clean, no matter how I wash them. They smell of other people's comfort, of warm skin and complacency, of slovenliness. Salt-sour with sweat and empty hours of not sleeping as he watches. The bed groans in protest as I try to find my place, then tries to spit me out before it swallows me whole. I wonder if you still sleep at home, in our bed, in the bed I made for us. I don't sleep. I force myself between the coarse blankets and shiver. Perpetual shivers that never escape the spine. A wave of unease that never breaks. Like a pecked kiss on the forehead of a corpse. Someone you'd loved. Shivers that don't end. Even through summer, caught up in the cloying grip of its cloth and steamed in my own sweat, I shiver as I evaporate. This bed makes nothing of me. This hateful bed. Sat squat before the dug-out. A giant upholstered roach at the mouth of a cave. Waiting.

The dug-out is carved directly into the cliff. Always dark, safe and solid. It's permanent, it's like it's always been here. A single bare bulb protrudes from the rock and offers some ailing light. Condensation gathers on the chain of its pull-switch, collecting at the end and dripping, intermittently, onto the wooden workbench below. The bulb was dead when I arrived. Its filament tinked inside the blown glass as I loosed the bayonet.

Small mineral islands flake the bench below the chain, interrupting its sheer patina. A residual archipelago. An imposing radio speaker stands over them. It looks old. It feels like it's from another time, like it's always been from before. It crackles to life at regular intervals. There's no way of measuring the time between. No need. Seconds, minutes, hours, they have no meaning here. Days are arbitrary at the cause. There are light times and there are dark times and there are the times that fall between. But I know that the voice comes regularly. I know that. I know the voice comes regularly. You can rely on the voice. I know the voice.

They say the voice is the first to go. From memory. That the voice is the first thing you forget. That when someone is lost it's their voice that follows first. I think about this carefully, speaking to myself as I do, so I don't forget my own. I remember you well, I think, because I remember your voice. I remember you singing quietly, always quietly, to yourself, like all the songs were just for you. I would listen, straining to hear them, for the pleasure of hearing you, you being you. The pleasure of being there at a moment when you were only yourself. I remember the way your voice would crack slightly as you reached for a chorus. And the idiosyncratic sounds you made when a lyric escaped you. When the words became not-words. But do I really remember your voice? Remember its tone? Its timbre? I remember the way you would say things, and I remember the things that you would say. But I can't hear you anymore.

It begins the same each time. A low hum emanates from the base of the transmitter, just audible. It bleeds into the room, becoming louder, gradually, gently vibrating the bench, gathering speed and violence until the whole cave hums. A harmony that wavers on the edge of hearing. The front of the box begins to glow as its inactivity thaws. A milky light, diffused by the pane of the transmitter's blind screen. Casting shadows harsh enough to reveal the pocked imperfections of the leather panels that encase it. The light gathers strength, like a spontaneous fire on a dry lawn, where the flames are hidden by the sun that started them, almost imperceptible until they're too strong to extinguish. The heat of the voice is hidden in this ambient warmth. It begins cold against the glow, a thin anonymous stream, but no less full and familiar for it. Its tinny tone remains somehow rich. Its remoteness is relatable. Obscure, but comforting. It describes the dangers we face and makes them real. It makes us ready. ... - *an unseen enemy is the most dangerous enemy of all* - ... It comforts. It reminds us of home, and of before. It reminds us that we are a 'we'. Binds multitudes of 'I's' together. *It* binds *us.* It reminds us that we are necessary. ... - *We require your strength, unity and cooperation to achieve our victory* - ... It explains our past so we understand it. Explains our past so we see our present as the path to our future. It makes it all make sense. Makes it sensible. The voice makes sense.

I began to think of the voice as his voice. It became the voice of the anonymous private. It called for vigilance and I obliged: patrolling diligently. It called for pride and I obliged: presenting arms to the injured trees. It called for strength and I obliged: I focus solely on myself. I am individually tuned, and never satisfied, and always becoming. I became what the anonymous private called for. I am.

Most of the food supply had been used, or taken, before I arrived. The same was true of medicine, first aid supplies, ammunition, and general hardware. There were a few tinned vegetables but they didn't last long and the experiments I made, planting beans from tins, all failed. I implemented a regime of foraging. A system of finding and learning. The water the causeway cut through was still and lifeless, it offered nothing, except the idea that I had arrived from somewhere else. The idea that there was somewhere other than here.

Sometimes that was the nourishment I needed.

To the right of the bunker was a pine forest. Uniform and airy, where the trees all presented in neat rows. It was a welcoming place, fresh, with a sharp light, even on dull days. A dry, sanitary and palatable place. Each tree swayed in time with the wind, always reaching toward one another but never touching. The pines offered little except resinous wood that I learned not to burn and hours of walking to nowhere. Their dropped needles were soft underfoot, comfortable and yielding, but always a bed of needles. Countless tiny deaths, singly sharp and hostile, combined in the illusion of compassion. But I enter the pines regularly, still seduced by the luxury they seem to offer. On warm days I close my eyes and turn my face skyward. The clouds scud above me and darken my eyelids like shoals of fish flitting between the spears of the trees. Sometimes, when I open my eyes, still blind in the sun, I think I see you, a red-green negative of you, or someone like you. Your outline. Before me.

To the left of the bunker was a mixed deciduous wood. Where no two trees were alike. The wood is fertile, but unforgiving. The trees simultaneously supporting and strangling each other. A persistent static violence in which the dead hold up the living. The wood quickly became impenetrable. The few trails I found, or hacked out for myself, were always too dark to follow for long. Knotted boundaries would always bar the way eventually. There, the limbs of the fallen and the living were so tightly enmeshed that it was impossible to tell one tree from another. Lichens competed along their boughs. Delicate fractals of bleached green and bistred orange, the living verdigris and rust of wood. The trees like the twisted remnants of some great shattered machine. It was around this point, the point that was impossible to pass, that foraging was best. I went there often, to the warmth of the place, to its generosity. It was there that I found sustenance. Blossoms, berries, leaves and bark, roots, nuts, and mushrooms. Mushrooms whose buff nippled caps teetered delicately on creamy stilts that ripened from the fetid earth. Its scent was warm and ostentatious, sweet in the nostrils but bitter in the throat.

The wood is unnerving. No false welcome like the pines. All still and quiet.

Nothing moves. No animals. No insects. No birds. Nothing. Even the wind holds its breath in the wood. The silence hangs thick in the air. A ballad to death. It tastes of gin, the silence, of juniper and bitter almonds. The bullet holes look on, blind and unblinking, offended by my presence. My movements insult a memory. Open old injuries. Awaken an atrocity that had insisted that time stand still. I return repeatedly. Dusk is the worst time. Dark sets so fast. The dusk just a fleeting glance from the day as it runs from the night. A stolen look over a fleeing shoulder. A look that says I'm sorry. I'm sorry I can't stay. I'm sorry to leave you. I'm sorry that you'll face the night alone. So I retreat as soon as the sun's resolve weakens. Back to the bunker. Back to the lonely chair and the crippled table. Back to the anonymous private. Back to the voice. To the static. To the waiting. To the waiting to begin again. This is my time. These are my days. A monotony of ritual. Rituals which fragment as they form routines. Collections of rituals. I am a soldier. I wait. I keep watch. I make repairs. I clean. I forage. I patrol. And I parade. I parade weekly. Infantry Private First Class, marching weekly for no one.

...

I woke up. The first fronds of sunlight were reaching in through the windows. Searchlights cutting through the room, illuminating the particles of dust which always floated aimlessly at that hour. A fly effervesced at the window. Its fat little body gives a plump-fingertip tap at the pane as it launches itself against the glass. Again, again, again-again, again, again. Rest. Again, again-again. Rest. A high tissue-comb-threnody of wings punctuates the tap-tap-tap and marks each take-off as it fizzes. Delicate compound eyes don't see the glazing that keeps them from freedom. I watch it. Rise and fall, rise and fall, rise and fall. The arc of its repetition reminds me of bubbles. Breaching the surface of a sparkling drink. And I'm submerged in memory, a cold lemonade, a flute of champagne. Returned, momentarily, to another life. A flute of champagne. A life before this one. A flute. There was music before. I hear it in the incessant confused buzz of those tiny confined wings. The music of before.

It was only much later that I realised. On a morning when the sun struggled to heat the land. The dew hung thick, clinging to its mother mist. A young doe ventured warily into the clearing. And I realised. The fly had been the first living creature I'd seen since my arrival at the outpost. The awkward grace of that young deer, each step so light, so carefully placed, and yet so precarious, made it all apparent. I watched and I realised. I'd danced in my bed with the fly. Held in early-light moments, an uneasy sleep still tugging at me, I'd waltzed through the melody of my nostalgias. I watched. Perfectly. Still. Awed by the stumbling elegance of her gait as it all became apparent. Birdsong, the whirr of insects, the dry distant crack of a twig. Like a rifle's echoed report. The ruffle of wings that accompanied it. The cause awakened around me. And when I moved, the grass fizzed at my feet. Crickets leaping clear. Effervescent.

After that I began to find strange freshwater oysters along the shoreline. And I remembered. I thought I remembered more. More clearly. I remembered the start of it all. The creeping rise. The unexpected victories. The belief. The net-curtain ghosts that enforced the early changes. Neighbour watching neighbour watching neighbour watching neighbour. Choosing sides. The shifts. The shift to us and them. I remembered the parades; the ordnance boom of the bass drum, heavy boots through streets, over them; the report of the snare above it. The loud speakers. Ejaculating ideas into crevices. Nestling safe between underdeveloped thought. And the flames, great tongues from sacred leaves. Language rising as smoke. Debate died. Truth went into hiding. Both replaced by impostors. Born of repeated lies. Life became singular. Monastic. Monolithic. Disagreement became dissidence. Then even the ghosts began to die. Dragged out from behind their hangings and forced to stand alone. The walls were stripped then spattered. The ropes ladened heavy with the burdens of the state. History was passed down upon us. A sentence of fate. A sentence that we all stammered through. I couldn't remember the side I'd chosen. I couldn't remember the principles I'd defended. I couldn't remember the people I'd fought beside. I couldn't see their faces. Or hear their voices. I couldn't remember. I cannot remember. I just cannot remember. But the voice reminds me.

Regularly. Repeating. ... - *an unseen enemy is the most dangerous enemy of all* - ... - *We require your strength, unity and cooperation to achieve our victory* - ... There was music before. We danced. My lips brushed yours, not quite a kiss. I buried my face in your shoulder. We laughed. I used to laugh.

The distance between then and now grows. Time is more ubiquitous. Less comprehensible. It can't mean what it used to. I want it to, I suppose. Only nothing stays the same. I wasn't always a soldier. I know that. But the memories of before are emptying out. They've become flat pictures. Pictures of places that no longer exist, or never existed at all. We took bikes into the village, through the small square by the harbour wall, the salt in the air stung our faces in the sun, the smell of fish frying and the patter of the locals, their dialect ricocheting about us, banking off the church walls, the bells peeling away the hours, chilled wine and cards, hot dice into the evening. But they are not there, and you are not there, and I am not there, and there is not there. It all empties out. All the joy and anticipation, all the anxiety and fear; until the only pain left is regret. The distance between then and now continues to grow. Only nothing stays the same. I am a soldier. I stand in my uniform. Dressed in ideals. In insignias that baffle me. Their meaning contingent to something I've lost. They represent an absence that has no meaning of its own. Still, I rarely stand naked. I am a soldier. With orders. But no army. I am alone. I don't remember what I am fighting. I don't remember who I am fighting. I don't remember why I am fighting. I am no longer fighting.

I was eating oysters when the jet flew over. Prizing them open with the tip of my combat knife, which I still sharpened daily. Severing the muscle that held their shells together. Swallowing them alive. They tasted of ozone and batteries. They tasted pure. They tasted of another life. I heard the plane before I saw it. A high nasal drone, constant and unapologetic. Its trail scarred the sky. An imprint. A two dimensional thing. Too high to have real form. Too far away to be the thing it was. But I understood it, and what it might mean. Anticipation coiled in me, my limbs were sprung, loosened by the tightness it invited. I thought of the pilot. Of another person. Another human being. I wonder if he hears the voice too. If it is the same voice. If we have that in common. The anonymous private. The plane passes. It's gone. The pilot never saw me. Never thought of me. Or, if he did, he never thought to return. I waited for him to circle. I watched the sky. Swifts moved above in greater numbers everyday now. Their warm liquid shrill elongated the dusk. The pilot never thought of me. The plane never returned. Then the symptoms began.

...

Confusion first. Questioning myself. Repeatedly. Unsure. Unsound. Always uncertain. Without recognition. I was in the dark. I sat in the dark. In the evening of my days. During the dark times. Has the bulb blown or have I forgotten to turn on the light? Inertia accompanied it. I would have tried the bulb. Now I sit; sat, sitting. Waiting for nothing. I can move, I think, but I don't. I have no will. I will not move. I wait for nothing. It feels better, easier, to wait. It's torture. I am content. I move. To gorge myself. Moved by a hunger, gnawing low in my pit. An emptiness that can't be filled. I consume mounds in shifts. I go through months of supplies in single sittings. Sharp berries that jar and bitter roots. Bowls of barely cooked mushrooms. Piles of them. Reconstituted, wet and resistant. Their purple-black gills greedily holding an oily sheen. I feel my gut taut. I am not satisfied. I am never satisfied. I drink pints. Gallons. Water, pickling brine, preserves. I gorge. I consume. I am consumed. I move only to get more. More. Mores. I waste. Excrete. Expel. I am waste. Dejecta. I am shit. I make no effort to move. I have no will. I will not. I shit and wallow in the earthy tang. Recline and float. Drift in a perfume of rejection. It floods my head. Headaches cast off from my sinuses, dull and heavy, an awkward small-talk of pain. They slosh and rattle about. Company for the confusion. Vicious memories that manifest, all rusted and barbed, in a porcelain skull that thins as they grow. They are agile and acute and incisive. They select points to attack then settle behind an eye, or both, with a pressure that makes me whimper before the blindness sets in. My skin tightens with fever. Shrinks around me as I crawl to my cot. The canvas webbing creaks as I dump my weight onto it. Its warp groans into the mattress as it reaches its limit. I feel my hair growing. Each follicle fighting to distance itself from my rancid scalp. I feel my nails getting longer. My teeth loosening as my gums recede. I screw my eyes back into my head. It's all I can do to hold my shape. And a nausea rises from the effort. A potent inevitability. The spit floods my mouth, overflows, great glooping strings of it, all stagnant and salinated. The heather mattress invites it on, its enticing urgency, tempered with moments of delay, of repression, of holding it all in place. Of fighting it. Beating it down. Repressing the relief.

Until. The first jerking spasm, the unavoidable purge, the contorted jets, streams of bile blasting through my head. Jets, jet, jet, again, again, again, again, again, again, again. Relief. Still. No calm. But still. Slight tremor in hand, silently conducting spent groans. I drip over the edge of the cot. I am sweat. I am tears. I am snot. I spit. Strings of bile stick to my chin. Acid. Taste it. Sour and ignorant. Drip; drip; drip. Caustic mucus in my throat. I need water. I need to wash out my head. I need. I have need. I have needs. I cannot. I am. No longer able to move. No longer will. I cannot move. I lie there. Unmoved. I lie. My eyelids twitch. Tic, tic, tic. Visions return. I cannot move. They are heavy. The lids. I'm trapped beneath them. It's dark. I lie. I am still here. But I'm slipping. Slipping between here and there. Where it is.

Whatever it was. I laugh. I dance there, still, sometimes. I am still here. The lids lift. It's light. The spotlights shift slowly across the room. Perfectly in time. They sweep the boards. Make feature stars of effluence. I am unmoved. I hear nothing. Ringing in my ears. Silent feedback. Post explosion. I smell nothing. My nose still full of my shame. The light in the room tinged green. I eye the windows. A lichen has grown between the panes of the portholes. The sun passes through it. Infuses the room with oxidised air. How long have I been here? I think. Knowledge of death becomes belief. Absolutely. The sound of it fills me. Lying there. At my lowest. Buoyant low-timbre of empty-full-drum. Thudding through me. It fills me at my lowest. When my lungs are completely empty. It brims, anxious and endless, and always starting over, always beginning again. And it begins again. The voice.

More regular than before. Repeating. Repeating. Repeating. Filling everything with words. The anonymous private. Speaking directly to me. Words. The tin-tone of the familiar. Whenever I am awake he is speaking. He is speaking. He is speaking. He is speaking. He is speaking to me. Everything that is is in his words. Everything he says is all that can be. His words are everything. The only words are the words of the voice. The voice is the only voice. The only voice is all voices. There are no other words. And even if there were, I could not hear them, or speak them, or write them. The voice goes on. I understand. I am moved. I know what I must do. The voice. I understand. The voice is my voice.

…

Words lose meaning. Relationships shattered. Their communion broken. I can no longer understand.

This must be a lie.
I lie here.
I'm lying here.

I tell the story. Retell the story. This must be a lie. The war is lost. This must be a lie. I am lost. This must be a lie. Lost to history. This must be a lie. I've lost sight of the end. This must be a lie. I've lost it.

Pulse bangs time in ear. March. Six eight time. We are outside. We find ourselves there. The sun is up. But the world isn't yet warmed. Our breath hangs before us. Grass whips bare legs. Trees bluster. Cold mud between toes. We pace through it. Gurgling. Consumptive. This isn't what you expected. The outpost has gone. The bunker is obliterated. We are naked. I'm only wearing my lips. You aren't here yet. We are naked and dry and cold and mobile. We are moved. We realise. Words realise. The words matter. The words are matter. The words are all that matter. We gambol toward the causeway. The clearing slips away behind us. Each step is dissolved. I sit by the shore. In the mud. In the sludge. I lie. Sink into it. Drawing warmth from around me. I look for the outpost. I face the past. The bullet holes in the trees have healed. Wet earth fills my mouth. Sapid clay. Mineral batter. I do not gag. I taste iron. I taste copper. Metallics replace shame. I'm breathing mud. Drinking and drowning. Accepting. Grit between teeth. Sands. Stones. Sediments. Seeds. Pits. My head is a shell. My tongue is an oyster. Grit becomes pearl. Pearl becomes word.

Everything changes.
Nothing stays the same.
There is nothing here.
It is beautiful.

GET OFF
Andrea Dandillot

I was first drawn to my Nemesis because he wore scuffed-up boots. He was already an entire head taller than me without shoes, but these boots gave him an extra two inches that he had no need for. They were made of a soft looking black leather and would have gone with anything, only they needed a thorough clean and polish. I have no reason to believe that this ever occurred to him, for he was completely at one with all of his affectations – as clichéd as they seem now. I may have noticed him in passing at registration but his image never became distinct until that day he walked in late to our freshman creative writing class. Narrow grey woolen pants and an untucked green dress shirt (which of course, needed to be pressed), completed his careless elegance. It was one of those bitterly cold but sunny New Haven mornings, and the heating in the room didn't work. He came and sat beside me, or at least he would have been beside me if there weren't an empty space between us. He never took his big blue overcoat off the entire time, nor spoke. He had pale brow eyes and the lids protruded ever so slightly; he scribbled constantly in his notepad, stopping only to occasionally grab handfuls of his longish messy hair. I remember being so transfixed by him that I lost track of what was being said. He looked as sad and wounded as I felt inside but wore it with arrogance – whereas I, consumed by an inevitable diffidence, could barely admit it even to myself. His sadness was so luxuriant, so extravagant that it had no regard for others. He didn't seem to suffer, even in sadness.

He only came back to that class one more time. This time I deliberately came in late, and made sure to sit right beside him. He looked up as I sat down and smiled, which made me uncomfortable. It didn't suit him, smiling. He had a battered copy of The Real Life of Sebastian Knight. Of course he did. And of course I asked him about it when class finished. He said he was going to get coffee, and plucking up all of my courage I asked him if I could join him. He looked at me oddly for what seemed like an aeon, and I felt so utterly humiliated that I wanted to cry.

'Of course.' He eventually replied.

He bought me coffee and we walked across the memorial quad and found a bench. He rolled a cigarette and started smoking. I asked him if I could get one, even though I hated smoking. He rolled it carefully in his long bony fingers. He talked about his parents, an English mother – working class, though, he insisted. Class was a sensitive topic, and one which I felt we shared – though in truth, it mattered more to him than me. He grew up in Rochester, and I was from Ithaca. It was crazy to me that there was someone like this who lived less than a hundred miles away from me, in that place that I had longed so much to escape. We talked about all the books he liked and all the books he hated, all of which, I commented, were by men. He apologized, and said he couldn't help what he liked. He told me that he wouldn't go back to the writing class. I told him it was naïve to assume that he already knew everything about writing at such a young age, that it's a skill to learn after all, and needs some work. He was almost two years older than me, having spent a gap year in Manchester looking after his maternal grandmother who had just died of lymphoma. He said that Nabokov once wrote that the only school of writing that exists is the school of talent, and he was convinced he had some talent. I told him I heard Nabokov got his wife to drive him all around America collecting butterflies, and that she typed up and checked all of his work. He said she was obviously a very patient and understanding woman. I said I also heard he cheated on her several times, once with a woman who groomed poodles. What does it matter what she did? He asked. I said it didn't, not really. He asked me if I liked his writing. I said I loved Lolita. Of course I did, he said. I also heard, I told him, that Nabokov ratted out Roman Jakobson to the FBI. He probably did, he replied: 'He did some terrible things. But they don't matter, in the end.'

Occasionally he would ask me questions, but I never volunteered much. He seemed too shy to maintain eye contact for more than a second and I was glad. The shyness was, I would learn, just another affectation. The wind picked up significantly, making the coffee cold in my cup, numbing my un-gloved hands and making my temples throb. He went into his rucksack and pulled out an old blue cable-knit sweater – and asked if I wanted to wear it. I pulled it on a little suspiciously. It had the smell of sweet musty cologne, and I wore it as I walked home to my dorm. I texted him to tell him I'd arrived home safely. 'Ok' he replied, and I felt like an idiot. Maybe that was the first time he made me feel that way, but it certainly was not the last. It wasn't intentional, just an inevitable symptom of his self-importance.

He lived in an apartment just off-campus which he shared with a philosophy grad student, a sullen but pretty woman named Meredith. I began spending a lot of time in his room. He never seemed to go to class, and apparently stayed up all night. He'd just be waking up when I came around in the late afternoon – he would make me coffee, and we sat around the living room reading together. He was usually in his pajamas and dressing down. I remember being both charmed and appalled that he actually owned a dressing down. Sometimes we'd read aloud to each other. He would often interrupt me when I was speaking and I would lose track of my own thoughts. He always stood up and paced the room whenever he read his own work, a cig dangling at the corner of his mouth. I would be reclined with my feet up on the couch in his bedroom, wearing more make-up than I usually wore to class. 'You're such a Capricorn it's not even funny', I'd tell him, and then attempt to giggle. He replied that astrology was bullshit. He had more than 'some' talent, and this must have been clear enough even to himself. He once told me that the Russians have two words that succinctly distinguish between a talented writer and a genius writer, a Turgenev and a Tolstoy for example, and at the time I was naïve enough to believe he belonged to the latter category – which was definitely what he wanted.

He wrote with an uncommon sensitivity which never came across as emotionally burdened, it revealed little of himself but communicated entire worlds with the strictest economy. He wore his stylistic influences lightly, but was nonetheless prepared to defend them against my flimsy critiques, which were unfit for purpose simply because I had neglected to read these men (and they were always men) as he had - if at all. No one has ever read my work as he did, nor since. He read with the utmost care but with a barely concealed boredom. His tepid and lazy appraisal of my work, universally lauded within the classroom, was the only one which I cared about. I began to write more and more with him in mind, and less with any trace of myself. Sometimes, in his most unguarded moments, he would begin to confide in me his various anxieties and neuroses, the causes of his anguish - and then, almost immediately, would stiffen, laugh it off and change the subject.

When he wasn't writing he was drinking, and always too much. I usually kept something back when I drank out of a need for self-preservation. In time, others intruded into our world and we found ourselves with friends who were not so much like-minded, but were at least inoffensive to our shared sensibility. Most thought themselves writers too, but were so in thrall to the trite pseudo-realism of the classroom that, really, they had no claim to our calling. We would all sit in dull bars, talk and drink beer. His presence commanded attention without seeking it, and this seemed to make him uneasy. The ebb and flow of conversation was modulated by his limited input;

people hung on his every word because there were so few, mistaking scarcity for profundity. It mattered little that what he said was usually mocking or so saturated with irony as to be utterly meaningless. He was not as forthcoming in public as he was with me in private.

One night in the bar, the talk turned to sex. Sex, for all of us, was only 'fucking.' Whenever it came up, we talked about who we'd fucked, or wanted to fuck – or the politics of fucking, and its various permutations and pitfalls. He contributed less than usual, and I sat to his side looking askance for tell-tale signs on his face. It's difficult to say what, if anything, I sought to find. During all those hours we'd spent in his room, sometimes we'd talk about love (too impersonally for it to be significant) but we'd never once spoke of fucking. Needless to say, I had never fucked anybody. I can only tell that I'm attractive because of the attention I would receive from men; attention that I never courted, and was largely indifferent to, but which he never expressed in any of the ways I had come to expect. But on that night, staring at his uncomfortable expression, I felt more than ever that I wanted to fuck him. I would drink far more than I ever had, and since we were celebrating a birthday, the night dragged on further. I made sure he never stopped drinking either. Soon we found ourselves edging closer through the hazy darkness, tremulous reverberations ringing in our ears, our friends nowhere to be found – I pushed my body into his, and he draped his arms around my waist and pulled me closer as our tongues mingled in a sickly serum of warm saliva and cold spirits.

And then we were back in his room, where I'd been so many times before – maybe imagining how this very moment would transpire. The din of the club still buzzing in my ear. I couldn't help but notice how different he now looked – the dark circles under his eyes, his hair wetted with perspiration, the entirety of his face resonant with a deep and uncharacteristic malice. He stood up, lifted me off my feet, placed me onto the bed and quickly removed my clothes and his own. He kissed me distractedly and briefly as he shoved his cock into me and began pounding away, burying his face between my shoulder and neck, grunting and breathing heavily. When he emerged I tried to look into his glazed-over eyes but he stubbornly refused – even in his inebriation - to reciprocate my hungry gaze. Everything was so numb in that moment that I barely felt any of the pain that would last for two weeks afterwards. In my mind I was begging for him to stop, to get off, and for it to be over – and it was, soon enough. He slid out of me, and within 10 seconds he was asleep. I wanted to fuck him, but he had instead fucked me – and therein, perhaps, was my primary grievance. But beyond fucking and being fucked was something else entirely and its absence is where my grievance acquired a certain pathos, which made our previous relations impossible.

I was, even at such a young age, more fatalistic than most. I avoided him as best I could afterwards – I ghosted him, let his calls ring out. I longed for him, nonetheless. Over those years, his image would flit across my various screens, and for a while I obsessively traced its course through life – even as my own seemed, in many ways, to be on hold. Then the image disappeared entirely from the internet, frozen in its youthful iteration. I stopped eating for the most part and neglected my medication - in private I sank into a maelstrom of anxiety and compulsive behaviour, yet remained diligent in my studies and was close to graduating top of my class. After some time there were other men, but each encounter was as abject as that first, or worse, far too banal to mention. The male mystique is non-existent, and if it does at first appear alluring – it quickly dissolves into thin air upon closer inspection.

Shortly before finals, I began to see him around again, with her, with Meredith. She must have been biding her time. He was, after all, only steps from her bedroom door – it must have been easy for her to entice him across the threshold. Beautiful and brooding Meredith, with her scholarly interest in professional philosophy, three years his senior, would provide him with all that he lacked. Like all men, he only wanted a mommy he could fuck. Despite never going to class, he somehow managed to graduate. I saw them once more before I left, at a table by the window illuminated by tense candlelight, as I walked past on my way home.

After the initial infection, the disease entered a period of latency. I moved to New York after college to take an internship at a literary magazine, which I had little difficulty making into an entry-level editorial job. For those first few years, I excelled in my work, and when I was suddenly laid-off – the reputation I had built for diligence meant I was re-hired at an adjacent publication within a week. More years passed where I made professional connections easily and seamlessly, and my narrative style of journalistic prose received the highest praise – but my ambition remained in fiction. Through the connections I had acquired, I secured a book deal to deliver a novel within two years. Of the several ideas I had previously wrestled with in college, none had so far coalesced into something that I felt warranted exposition. I wrote everyday about politics, culture, and sex (still 'fucking') and extrapolated on the primacy of lived experience, but in truth, my experience of life was limited. I stubbornly chose to live alone in a tiny one bedroom I could barely afford, and although I was active and engaged online, I had only a few close friends IRL - none of whom I felt I could ever trust completely, nor confide in entirely, other than in those drunkenly performative but ultimately meaningless ways. I rarely went out. My private anxiety, which had no real outlet, manifested itself in various peculiar and pathological habits; I kept food diary, which informed me when it was expedient to starve myself, and an exercise diary for when it was appropriate to punish myself. Interesting as such emotive and topical pathologies were to the current moment, I knew all too well that they amounted to nothing more than trite cliché.

I began only dating women, which I took to without much ceremony. Almost overnight my personal life seemed to thrive, and, after a few false starts – I found myself in a long-term relationship with a woman named Nomi. Overtime, some of my sharp edges began to soften and I began to feel more at ease with others and myself. She was a writer, like me, but her convictions were more profound than her talent, which was interchangeable with those of her contemporaries. I often admonished myself for judging someone whom I cared for so deeply in such an unforgiving light. She felt strongly that the purported genius of men came at the expense of women's erasure; but in her case, it could not help but feel like a consolation. I came to realize that I was temperamentally incapable of reciprocating her authentic feelings of solidarity. Try as I might, I couldn't reveal much of myself to her.

And then one day I saw him, my Nemesis, on the L train. I had been working later than usual, and he got on at Union Square. The carriage was crowded, and I was sitting down with my head bowed over my phone. At first I saw the boots – I couldn't tell if they were exactly the same pair (they certainly looked similar) but the way they were scuffed was difficult to mistake. He looked different; more gaunt and haunted looking, with longer hair – but the eyes had remained unchanged. He was dressed entirely in black, with a hood pulled up over his head. It looked as if he hadn't slept in a week. He never noticed me, and I missed my stop. Eventually he got off at Jefferson Street, and I got off too without thinking. I dragged my feet and walked well behind him. I followed him home. From the opposite sidewalk, I watched him going into a four floor. I had known at the back of my mind that he was living in the city – even his absence was always palpable – but for those first few years I never saw him around. Eventually I pieced together his presence bit by bit from the ether; I found myself lurking on the accounts of his friends and co-workers, trying to put together the different faces and events that composed a life which was being lived in proximity to my own, but detached from it entirely. It was clear that Meredith was no longer around. He didn't seem to have stable employment – bar jobs, retail and short term positions in various failed literary ventures on the peripheries. He lived alone as far as I could tell, and I suspected he may also have been selling drugs to make rent - an occupation practiced with impunity within a certain demographic in this city. I began staying at the office later and riding the L-train at around the same time each day. Over the course of three months I spotted him several times, always making sure to keep my distance. He'd probably struggle to recognize me; my hair was blonde and I'd become dramatically thinner. I wore a baseball cap just in case. At the beginning he'd get on at Union square and get off at Jefferson Street. After a while, he began getting on at Bedford Avenue and getting off at Myrtle Wyckoff. And then, after a while, he disappeared. I continued for a couple more weeks, but since I had recently moved into Nomi's apartment in Bed-Sty, the added commuting time was starting to draw suspicion.

Soon afterwards, I was invited to the annual party thrown by the magazine's editor-at-large. He was an erstwhile writer of transgressive 90s fiction, now mellowed, who still attempted to cultivate a bad boy persona (patchy facial hair, flannel shirts with rolled sleeves to display his awful tattoos), despite standing at 5ft 7, and hailing from a Midwestern construction money. His voice remained boyish and effete, despite his fifty odd years. He spoke entirely in the platitudes of the creative writing classroom, which he had scarcely left as a student before being appointed as professor almost two decades ago. In his over-sized and overfilled West Village apartment he held court (as he liked to think), over a captive audience of precarious staff exclusively composed of young women. 'I spent my entire career championing women writers', he would proclaim, and as the night progressed – he would try to pick each of us off, whispering what he took to be flirtatious suggestions into compliant but resistive ears through his alcohol soaked breath. He cornered me as I came out of the bathroom. He told me that he'd always wondered what it would be like to fuck me, and assumed an expression which suggested that his use of profanity was enough to entice anyone to partake of the implied offer. I told him I only dated women. I contemplated this puerile little man, with his dorky tattoos, doughy body and complete lack of any naturally fuckable qualities, but who fucked nonetheless. He did so because of his ostensible 'talent', but in reality because of a much more tangible and less rarefied power. What was most egregious to me was that this power wasn't sought, but conferred. He couldn't have been unaware of this, but gladly accepted its advantages – a string of ambitious and self-obsessed young women consenting to be defiled by his shriveled mediocre cock. Later that night, I gave him a dry hand-job in his guest room while I waited for my Uber. After cumming he became morose:

'You know, I've spent my entire life championing women writers…but they've like, completely ruined writing. There's nothing that attempts to grasp at the sublime, man. All writing's confessional writing now, personal, overly emotional – it's all histrionics, suffering, bodies, spaces and all this other bullshit.'

'Écriture féminine', I replied

'Huh?'

'Nothing….my Uber's here.'

On the way home I cried epiphanic tears in the certainty that I had finally found my subject. The subject was suffering, or more precisely, the lack of it. My Nemesis hadn't disappeared completely, and I would see him again. Over the years he had continued to write, my Nemesis. Despite the lack of recognition, despite the frequent and discouraging rejection, lack of money and passing modes resistant to his own - he had honed and matured a distinctive prose style which I carefully traced through various short stories in publications varying from the obscure to the obscure enough to be respected. I pored over these stories, but couldn't seem to suture together any sort of coherent view of his psychic life; the presence of an overbearing and violent father, perhaps, but a distant and indifferent mother also. None of it cohered, and seemed to come up short when presented with the final result, which was invariably brilliant. I skulked in the shadows of a reading my Nemesis once gave, and to which I'd brought Nomi along as if on a whim. He had what looked like a black eye, his delivery was low and almost mumbled. The audience was comprised entirely of thirsty young women, who keenly approached him one by one afterwards. He left alone. I learned from some sources that he had been given a small book deal, and was working on a novel. This discovery provided me with the necessary impetus to intensify my own efforts. If suffering was the theme then equality was its inescapable mode of expression: men needed to suffer, in order to be equal to our suffering. The inequity of suffering, expressed in the most vital and evocative prose – a prose that speaks in words, without looking to sentiments. I began to work more obsessively than I'd ever worked before – I'd come home from work and work until 3am most nights, sleep for 4 hours and then go back to work. I worked weekends, holidays and through one brief European vacation; I neglected to eat, I neglected to work out, and I neglected her. We broke up – and I moved out on my own again, into a cramped studio in the Lower-East Side. I continued to work, working until I felt delirious with anticipation. I took an entire month off work to push it over the finish line during a time when my job had become insecure due to restructuring. And then it was done. Haggard, aged, completely run-down and on the cusp of potential unemployment – I triumphantly handed over the manuscript. Within six months, I was holding the first copies in my hands.

...

It was my most cherished achievement. The reviews were full of admiration and near universal praise. Several breathless articles in succession, and in different but related ways, pointed towards the publication of my work signifying a paradigm shift. My life changed dramatically as I became more and more in demand. I gave readings in London, Dublin and Berlin; I was a guest panelist on campuses around the country, I was given my own column, and a new two-book deal that came with a hefty advance. Despite all of this, there was a lingering discomfort. The appraisal of my work was generous but facile;

its reality had been rendered obsolete in favor of its status as a conduit for ideas that had not even occurred to me when writing. This was the most real thing I had ever created, but it was almost as if its reality was too suspect, too inconvenient and frightful to bear. Alternate, more palatable, realities were superimposed over my own. These thoughts lingered, percolating in my innate self-doubt, until I had all but convinced myself of the unvarnished truth; no one had properly read my book, and it would have been better if it hadn't been read at all.

...

One afternoon, I was walking home from the F train and stopped in the café down from my apartment. Recently, I'd been struggling to fill my column with half-way interesting insights, and had started to basically phone it in. I had been putting off writing it up until the deadline, which was that night, so I got coffee and sat at a table by the window. Huddled over my laptop I could sense a shadow looming over me. I looked up.

'Andrea'

'Oh my god no way'

He looked a little more put together, now; shaved, rested, and dressed almost presentably. A solitary grey hair drooped carelessly from his crown, and that was all that attested to the passing of time; the both of us just past thirty − but he looked no different from that first time we met in class. I had changed completely − whilst still feeling the same. He sat down with me and we fell into easy conversation, as if the intervening years had not even occurred. I couldn't be entirely sure that they had. He had read my book, and he couldn't stop talking about it. And what's more, a fact that I still can't seem to grasp − this man, my Nemesis, had read it in exactly the way that it should have been read. He spoke in precise terms of its intricacy, its subtlety and (most importantly) of its reality without any recourse to facile praise; he had read it for it was, in its entirety. He had read it, and had found it lacking. He never said as much, exactly, but I had long ago learned how to read him. I could barely contain my rage, but as ever, managed not to let on. We arranged to meet the next night.

I prepared for what was to be our final reckoning by channeling all of the methods I had accumulated to make myself desirable and attractive, without really knowing why. I preened, plucked, polished, and painted until my whole body felt entirely apart from myself. I made my way through the night, clad in an imperceptible armor, floating on a cloud of perfumed vapor, vengeful, delirious and ravenous. I arrived to an almost empty bar, dimly lit, with him nursing a bourbon cocktail in one of the corner booths. He looked up at me as I approached in a way that was wholly unfamiliar, a prelude to the uneasy conversation that followed. The first hour was punctuated by awkward pauses, and a smattering of small talk. I left my card open at the bar, and we drank in relative silence together for a while until he steadily became a little more animated. He had, it transpired, completed his novel and had that very afternoon handed over the manuscript to his publisher, a small independent press. It would, in all certainty, disappear without a trace into a world thick with words, which no one was either capable, or willing, to read. He seemed unmoored and introspective. I hadn't reckoned with having to drive things forward, and it took some adjustment on my part to take the initiative. I hadn't come to talk, after all.

'What's the premise of your novel?' I asked abruptly.

'If I only talk about the premise, then I won't be describing it.' He replied.

'Can't you summarize it for me?'

'I'm not sure I can.'

'Well, what's it about?'

'It's about love, among other things.'

'That's not very original.'

'I guess not.'

'You say it's about love…but it's probably just about yourself.'

'Why do you think that?'

'It's just a hunch…I feel like, going by my experience of men writing about love, it never extends beyond their own vanity.'

'…but I feel like it's not just about me.' He said, a little exasperated.

'But what do I know?' I replied with an involuntary snort, 'I've never been in love.'

'…'

'What's your process? How do you work?' I demanded, attempting to deflect.

'What work?'

'Your writing.'

'I just write, it either comes or it doesn't – but it never feels like work.' He said, a little dejectedly.

'I find that hard to believe. If it isn't work, then it isn't worthwhile. But then again, the assumption is that it just comes from nothing - people don't expect you to work in the same way.'

'Well, maybe you're working too hard.' He suggested, somewhat distracted.

'That's not it….'

There followed an extended silence during which he did his best to avoid eye contact. After a while, he was thoroughly drunk, slurring his words slightly and yawning. I began to talk, at first just to fill up the space. But once I had begun – I found that I couldn't seem to stop; a torrent of words burst forth, barely articulated before colliding with others. I extrapolated on my life thus far, my failures and triumphs, and, with the most minimal prompting – I found myself amidst the innermost territory, surprised by how quick the journey was. I kept back only those things it was impossible to reveal, and with every revelation I began to feel simultaneously unburdened and confined, as if floating a couple of feet above a prison yard, dwarfed by a twenty foot prison wall. The more I spoke, the more I could sense his mounting shame. Eventually I stopped speaking, and sunk back into my seat, my eyes filling with tears which it took all my strength to hold back. I knew that it was impossible to say what I really needed to say, and at any rate, I had no idea what it was. I abruptly got up to leave, but he stood up at the same time. Before I knew it – he was embracing me, holding me firmly to his chest. For a brief moment, I felt the world was in stasis, calm and placid – but when it was over, the familiar feeling of dissonance returned.

I realized when we got out onto the street that he was barely able to walk. I took him to his apartment in Ridgewood. I supported him up the stairs, almost carrying him the last few steps. It was a studio with an old couch, a desk, a double bed, and a small bookcase. I eased him onto the bed, pulled off his shirt, pants, shoes and socks. I got undressed and lay down beside him under the blankets. He turned onto his side, facing me, looking right into my eyes. 'I'm glad you came back', he said as he closed his eyes and drifted off to sleep. After five minutes, he moved onto his back and began snoring loudly. I nudged him in his side with my elbow and he turned back to face me and stopped snoring. I lay awake beside him, watching him sleep, until 5am. I got up, got dressed and went home.

A week before his novel was published; they retrieved the bloated body of my Nemesis from the Gowanus Canal, his coat pockets filled with stones and gravel. There was no note as such, but a few torn up index cards found at his place, with certain words crossed out, seemed to be proof enough. At first, his death registered merely as a few passing comments amid the chatter, condolences shared amongst those he knew, performative grief enacted online and immediately forgotten - because to be online, is ultimately to forget. But somehow he wasn't completely forgotten. A memorial fund-raising page raised $2682. And then nothing, for a year or so. Eventually a new edition of his novel was published by a bigger press, and an anthology of his short stories with an introduction by a prominent and respected scholar followed. Both sold well, and were reviewed with reverential tones in every publication that still bothered to discuss literature. Inevitably, once the word 'great' had been uttered – the word genius was usually not far behind. At first it was used cautiously and sparingly, but in time, and in retrospect, as the texture of the work became inseparable from the tragic fate of the author, it became standard. I was asked to review it in my column and agreed.

I sat down at my desk and opened a new document. I wasn't exactly sure what to write. The book was about love, he was right. But as hard as I tried, I couldn't separate the lives which the work sought to depict with the little I could surmise of his own. It was less than the sum of its parts. Moments of penetrating psychology, haunting imagery and sublime beauty were combined with extended periods of the most infuriating banality, overdetermined and underwhelming. It was a book of sensations and sensuality, and in consequence, over-indulgent. The book was about love, and it was about a woman – a woman who appears early and in passing, but to whom I discovered many oblique references hidden throughout the text. Early on he betrays her, and she is incapable of forgiving him. But her aura permeates the work - her world-weary philosophy informing, in its way, all of his subsequent actions. His thoughts continually return to her, even through his numerous encounters with other women who bring him nothing but chaos and antipathy – traits that his masochistic ego seemed to court. And then there were others, women whom he did not desire – but whom he seemed to cherish all the more, because he could exact his revenge on them for all the others. His magnum opus, the sum all of his purported genius, amounted to so little that it made me angry. The petty consolation of its subject matter and the truth of his feelings for me, could not assuage the impression I had of being cheated. And, in the end, was that it? Nothing of my actual self will remain, just as nothing of what he described will ever correspond to a reality never fully acknowledged. Even a painful and untimely death could not make him suffer. All he had to do was leave, to never speak again, to transcend his own mediocrity. All he had to do was die. Is my only recourse, then, to go on living? I sighed heavily as I reached for the keys in anticipation.

IF I COULD BE ME ONE LAST TIME, I WOULD BE YOU

Leah Case

There are two ways to get a new body. The first is to die: to take what you are thrown back into and to deal with it. The second is to be so rich that cost is an adjective of abstraction, not a barrier.

And what if you don't get what you want? Again and again and again and *again*. What if that body is never *you*?

Well, then you're twelve.

No, not years.

Cycles. Iterations. Reincarnations. Whatever.

You're twelve and you're me and you're told this is your last one, so make the best of it.

"Why?"

"What do you mean, why?" The technician looked perplexed at my question, irises dilating and clicking as they brought me into sharper focus. "Everyone has a last. This one is yours." He then took the tether from the base of my skull, a quick snap breaking the link from my back-up. I felt alone.

And once again, this wasn't the body I wanted to be left with. Two months of limbo and a slowly deteriorating sense of self for this: a dozen digits, straight-faced, and stubble peaking through like knives to shred me from inside out.

"Make the best of it," he said again.

...

I got a tattoo that night and found out the pain receptors of this body were amped up to eleven. Every single moment of it was a scream—sharp, prolonged, but a reminder that I was alive. So I persisted until butterfly wings made themselves known on plastic skin stretched over titanium shoulder blades, and planned for the ellipse across my belly; the map down my thigh; the wave on the soon-to-be shaved side of my head.

When you're given a new body, it's actually winning the lottery. No, you're not the winner. Someone else is. A First who'd put their name down had died and been chosen to represent the latest batch of lives for anyone who is sequential. You can only choose how long you wait to be reinserted into something more desirable.

The criteria are few, though: one is race, the other is gender. Though race is on its way out, people say.

"It's barbaric," you've heard said a dozen times. But it's also on a form written a few millennia ago, so—you know. Bureaucracy.

No one seems ready to let gender go, though. Least of all me—I'm sorry. I know, I should be better than this. But least of all me.

So, it's never quite what you want, and certainly not something you might identify with. They just ship out two thousand models every two weeks of the latest winners and you hope it's good enough.

Choosing to hold two weeks is fine. "Negligible chance of loss of cognitive form and function," the information packet says. At a four-week hold it says, "Potential for small loss of cognitive form and function." At six weeks it says, "Expect some loss of cognitive form and function." At eight weeks it says, ***"WARNING: COGNITIVE FORM AND FUNCTION WILL BE LOST."***

There is no ten-week hold.

Most people learn to make compromises, to make changes, and to say, "I'll get something better next time," because we've made an industry of Buddhism where the next life is supposed to be Nirvana, but there's no one keeping score. Bodies are not meant as rewards or punishment, they're just pulleys and pistons and a facsimile of self. It's posthumanism and it's hell.

Would I get piercings this time? The tattoo still stung as I rode home, leaving me unable to lean back against the vellum-esque seats of the train. But the answer was yes. It was always yes. I wanted myself to be a scream and for the body I was given to be a whisper.

Which was all a waste of time—everyone *got* it. I was just the idiot who decided to care, and fuck you for thinking I should get over myself and *settle*. It's my life. My body. And now this is my last because if I go for one more round, they expect my mind will be more a shell than my body. That's where they draw the line between post-human and in-human. Too many memories and mannerisms lost to cold storage, waiting for the body that will never come.

I was barely halfway home when I started grasping an idea, though I kept it to myself.

...

"This is the last one," I said, kicking my shoes off in the front hall. It was late, but I'd been dead for two months, so Damian and Rain were up and waiting. I put dented wall as I tried to take off my shoes standing with this unfamiliar balance, toes lacking dexterity or agency.

"Wait—no. How?" Damian raised spindled arms like weapons of exasperation. "You're just twelve!"

"Why do you think?"

"You're still you," Rain said. "You've done nothing to deserve this."

They were thirteen and fourteen respectively, and twelve cycles ago, they had been parents to my First. Now they were just roommates who'd need a new renter for their last two or three cycles.

"There's nothing wrong with you," Damian said.

"Probably think I'm irresponsible, if nothing else." Four bodies in two decades wasn't great—and with that eight-week wait for each new one, who knew who I was anymore.

"Can you appeal?"

"Can you help me with this?" I took off my shirt to reveal the red, slightly bloody back I now bore. There was some aftercare I had to do before going to bed. Rain took the bag with the lotion. While she had no tattoos, she'd helped with mine often enough to know the procedure.

The back had a shaved smooth square with a tangled frame around the tattoo—even for a male-form, this body was hairy. A lot like my first one, though anything I remembered from that was purely second-hand. Ninety years of being told, "Just you wait. It only gets better," for it to be proven wrong.

Rain applied the lotion, and while I did my best to ignore screaming pain receptors, the way this body twitched at every touch was beyond my control. It had almost made the tattooist refuse to continue.

Finally, with my shirt back on and hanging loosely against sore flesh, I said, "I'm going to bed." It was way past midnight, and I felt like the kind of shit that required sleeping facedown for fourteen or sixteen hours.

"Are you sure you don't want birthday dinner?"

"I'm sure."

This body didn't like to sleep on its stomach, though, and it took five or six nights of too-little rest before I reached something that approximated comfort between raw skin and silk sheets.

...

The rest of the tattoos caused fewer problems. The first piercing got infected, but I caught it quickly, and the doctor only threatened to cut the ear off and replace it with plaster momentarily before prescribing antibiobots. She said, "You should be more careful."

And I said, "Yeah," an hour before my appointment for the hip dermal. Which hurt and, as ever, had a diamond tip that caught on everything. One day, the tip screwed off entirely and after thirty minutes of watching my twitchy, pudgy digits fail, Damian offered to help with his feminine fingers.

He never seemed to mind other bodies much. He just went with the standard little tag to signal his identity and then moved on with his life. He could wear breasts like they were pecs and make the grit he overlaid on any soprano sound unforced.

"Firsts get to fuck around with their bodies all the time. There's a whole industry for it," I said.

Damian was eye-level with my hip, staring intently as he held the diamond tip between index finger and thumb of one hand and kept the barb in my plastic skin steady with the other. It only hurt a little. "Yeah?"

"Yep. You say, 'I hate my body,' and then someone else says, 'Okay, let's see what we can do.'"

"Mhmm." He started twisting, but he'd squeezed the skin wrong and the barb slapped the tip from his fingers. He scrambled to retrieve it before it was lost to a corner of the room.

"Mostly just some hormones. Estrogen. Testosterone. Some blockers. It's all so *civilized*."

He was back at my hip. "Sounds like it."

"So why can't *we* do that?"

"Because we don't have receptors for them?"

I sighed. "I didn't mean literally. Why not split batches? Why not guaran—guaran—guaran—guaran—guaran—guaran—guaran—guaran—guaran—FUCK!" Even after I abandoned the thought, my twitching wouldn't stop, forcing Damian to pause his efforts.

"Well, that is the question. But I don't know. You can still just pay for what you want."

"Yeah. Let me go fork over a million bucks to get it."

"Maybe you'd have enough now, if you'd saved."

"Thanks. That helps."

The twitches subsided. The bit threaded itself, and after a few swift turns, it was on.

...

Damian was being hyperbolic when he said I'd have enough money if I'd saved. Yes, maybe if I'd saved *every* dollar since I was born without experiencing a moment of pleasure in twelve bodies, I'd have enough for one of my own. Pleasure allowances were small, and mine were saved for times like now when I had to start over again and define myself in fresh terms on fresh skin and fresh blood, recycled through generations of other bodies.

There are no surgeons for sequentials. There might've been black markets, I don't know. I was too scared to ever try anything that wasn't government sanctioned, even after all this time. It's one warranty not worth making void.

I showed up to my job, let the body go on autopilot for its eight-hour shift, then resurfaced and persisted with my existence in the off-hours.

But this was my last one. This was my last one?

My last one.

My *last* one my last one my last *one* my last one *my* last one.

My. Last.

One.

I pulled myself together rather than pulling my jaws apart to stifle the stupid noises I was making as I repeated those words over and over and over in my head on the way home. The realization that I would do anything (legal) to make sure this was not my last was so overwhelming that it felt like being hit by the train I rode.

...

A few days later when I was depressed and home alone, I got the reply on my posting that I had been waiting for. I went to meet her immediately.

She couldn't leave home any longer. One-hundred-and-ten years old and hanging on to the bitter finish. There was a respirator, three chemical drips, and enough pill boxes scattering her bedside to confuse a supercomputer. A bored sequential body on their dayshift let me in with blank eyes and a nod.

"I get the emotive ones in the evenings." The breathing was mechanical, spaced between words through a tube drilled in her throat. "When I'm asleep. Take a seat."

It took a bit of doing to accomplish. The room was cluttered in a way only Firsts could manage, so full of *self* that it seemed like she lived more in the apartment than the body. The chair was a relic showing years if not decades of wear underneath a few folded blankets, which I moved. A TV on the wall was playing a nature documentary about de-extinction, the world around it cluttered with holos and knick-knacks and one fist-sized hole so old that the surrounding stained blood was black and nearly all flaked away. A tabletop made of moonrock was scattered with souvenirs from at least fifty different countries and two different planets.

"You've come a long way," I said.

"And there's nowhere left to go."

"You're sure?" I had to push. I couldn't let someone so young make such a large mistake because of me in good faith. "You never know what the next life might bring."

"This is the only me I've ever needed to be. What could be better than this?" She gestured down at her frail body, which was breaking out in pained sweats. "I'll die before I end up like you." It was a joke, maybe, her limbs possessing this palsy that I would have thought unbearable, if I were not sitting across from her with two twitches to match every one of hers.

That was good-enough faith.

\#

I understood where she was coming from. Despite everything, my First was probably the closest I ever got to… Me. At least according to the photos—the memories of what it felt like are labeled **VOID**.

Coming home from work one day, I'd tried once to dredge up the earliest memory of knowing my body was wrong—the horror that *surely* must have existed during that first puberty—but as I began to convulse in my seat and slip to the floor of the train car, all I got were these lukewarm feelings of discomfort overlaid the fuzzy, distorted image of legs in a bathtub. A push further blacked out my vision, concerned travellers disappearing into nothingness as I was gifted a lightning flash memory of staring at an armpit, then—

I was at the hospital, a doctor telling me there was nothing they could do: the entire First archive had been resected before it corrupted any adjacent files. A few days later, Rain had frowned and said, "You seem different," and I was too afraid to ask, "In what way?"
I'd had four female bodies. There was this beautiful period—*two in a row*. I'd forgotten that anything had been wrong, even though the person in the mirror was never quite me. But that was fine when I hid her behind the piercings and the tattoos and the personas I tried on like hats. Maybe I was the kind of girl to do this, or to do that.

But nothing ever stuck. Try being a woman for the first time at three hundred. Try laughing with someone on the train when she says, "I'm glad sequentials don't have periods. They were awful, weren't they?" because it's hard to admit that even when she says it in a gravelly bass-deep tone through an unkempt beard, she knows more than you ever will about the useless gash you've waited so long to have between your legs.

By then I started to realize that maybe it was just a problem with me—not like my brain was synapses and hormones or whatever the hell else. It's an atomic clock of either/or states so clean-cut and precise part of me refuses to believe they can ever define being human, which has always seemed to be either/and.

Rain liked to take a new name with each new body. "It's a fresh start," she told me once. "I don't see a point in not moving on. Otherwise, I'll just be living the same life over and over again." She'd stopped being my mother nine or ten cycles before that.

"You can keep the same name," I said.

She shrugged. "But I don't have to. So just call me Rain now, okay?"

"Okay." No back talk from me; I wasn't on my first name either. Still, I was young and in my tenth body at that time, Rain just at the start of her fourteenth. Damian had gone out to pick her up her birthday meal—chicken fried rice. "Why do you care about the gender, then? Would it be easier for you to just change that too?"

She raised an eyebrow. "Would it be easier for you?"

"No," I said. "But I'm wondering if it would for you. There's only one me I've ever wanted to be, and I haven't gotten her right yet."

"That sounds like a fool's errand. You'll never be as good as you want to be. As cool as you want to be. As *you* as you want to be. You're just the you you are now. Nothing less, nothing more." She was limbering up her new body—female-form, pretty. She'd cut her hair close to the skull on the way home since new bodies came with a full two feet of hair otherwise.

"Thanks for the wisdom, but I can at least try, can't I?"

"Definitely. It just kinda sounds like it sucks for you."

I shook my head. "That's why I'm trying."

She shrugged, or maybe it was just her next stretch. The body was the kind you could be anything with, its shape vague and malleable. An arm swung in wide circles, the occasional *pop* sounding from a shoulder. "Chicken or egg."

Then the door opened, and there was Damian's bulky form. Like a Valkyrie in the feast halls of Valhalla. "Who's hungry?"

\#

The First's name was a bit classical, almost out of touch with her sensibilities. Katrine. All she talked about was "what comes next." What it must be like to leave the solar system, all that kind of stuff. I almost told her to have her next body be somewhere else. It was more than within the realm of possibility, but she'd made her decision, so I let the point slide.

"I'm glad there was pushback against that 'live inside a computer' crap. It just wouldn't be the same," she said. "At least when you're out here, you can pretend what goes wrong with your life isn't really anybody's fault. In there you'd know there was someone at fault, someone could change it, and you'd probably have their email address."

"And they still wouldn't change it," I said.

"And they still wouldn't," she said and made an approximation of a nod. The tube in her throat didn't allow for much movement, though the dayshift sequential moved her every now and then. "Now, is it my body you want, or my life?"

"I want to be real. Just once."

"What have you done until now—whose life have you been living? Why is *my* body the vehicle you need?"

"It just is," I said. "You're ready to die because I bet you can't imagine how a next life could possibly be any more *you* than you've been for the last hundred years. I've lived your life a dozen times over, and I couldn't tell you who I've been once throughout it all. Only who I've tried to be."

"Why can't you be it in there?"

"Could you?"

"Wouldn't want to."

"There's your answer."

"I didn't say that I couldn't."

"Well, I can't." I made a broad gesture at the body. "It's not for lack of trying."

"Mine won't be any different," she said. "It won't be perfect. Do you want just to be pretty? Fuckable? Because I've never even been either." Her laugh was throaty and gross. "If this is what a thousand years of insecurity looks like, I'll be glad not to have it."

"Just sign or don't. I'm not going to sit through you being a bitch for nothing."

"Oh, I'll sign." She held up a shaky hand for a pen. "I just can't imagine in what world this will give you what you want."

"Yeah, well, that's because you've always had it." I put the pen into her hand with far more roughness than I should have, but she took it without complaint. Signed. Bid me a terse goodbye that I scarcely cared to return.

What we did was kind of a loophole, kind of an abuse of the system. Something they assumed most people wouldn't care about and something that would be patched once—if—I did it. Whatever. I just wanted my one last time.

I would not die in this body. I would not die a failed human. If I had my way, I would be inhuman in whatever way possible.

Now I just had to wait for Katrine to die.

"Any day now," she'd said as she'd signed with those failing hands, gripping the pen as if her fingers might break.

"I'm sure you'll have many ahead of you," I said.

"But hopefully not too many."

I shrugged. She finished the two-letter signature and dropped the pen, laying back to let her tube pant. The nature documentary on the TV was about indigenous Martian plants now, making the screen look a bloody red.

...

A month later, I was still in this body.

A year later, I was still in this body.

Two years later, I got a note from Katrine that initially made my heart jump, oily sweat incongruous on cool skin. It said, "Sorry. I promise I'm getting around to it, but I'm down South." Attached was a picture of her—tube and wires and drips intact—on a mountain slope in some sort of artificial globe. She appeared asleep and smaller for all the new wrinkles.

"Take your time," I replied, and that evening I accidentally bit the body's nails until an index finger was left raw down to the quick. It never grew back quite the same. One of a million minors scars I collected.

It always seemed to happen that way, apart from the piercings, apart from the tattoos, I always acted as someone who didn't *quite* grasp that they might experience consequences for their actions.

The joints of my jaw began to catch and click, coming out of alignment from all the time I spent chewing those nails. It was a habit I told myself I'd lose with every new body, and every time I failed. Looking at Katrine, and really any Firsts, I asked myself how much those first few years defined … everything afterward. Maybe if I still had them I'd know.

Was I going to die before Katrine did?

. . .

I severed an arm coming back from work one day. Yeah. Lots of blood, lots of pain. Stopped the trains for hours. In the end, they blamed it on a mechanical fault. Of all the stupid things to ever happen to me, I found it hilarious that that wasn't my fault. I'd been in a hurry, frustrated and twitchy, and the doors had been closing and caught an arm as I slid inside. No, the doors were gentle on my faux-flesh. It was the first concrete pillar we passed that was rough.

It wasn't all bad, though. Seriously. They don't keep replacements of each body batch, and I'd never been so happy for that.

I got a new arm. Slim. Mostly hairless, and entirely in conflict with the rest of my body. Even the skin tones were off, though they did try to match that sort of thing. I lost the tattoos the arm had had—a flower, a knife, the words 'You Will Know Me' in an ink-blotted type—but what I was left with felt so much better.

I cried the first time I saw it, and the nurse asked, "Do you need more painkillers"—she stopped to check the tag I wore—"miss?"

I held the arm to me like a newborn (not that I could ever possibly experience that—this had to be enough [was this really all I'd get? {Why? (Why? [*Why?*])}]), and said, "No, thank you."

One more day and I was out of the hospital, an unimpressed Damian and worried Rain waiting for me with a dinner of garlic fried shrimp at home. It had been my favourite. But, as usual, the joke was on me. I took one bite and gagged, almost threw up then and there on the table. I managed to let the half-chewed shrimp fall out of my mouth without the bile pushing at my throat.

"Oh." Rain frowned. "I thought these were your favourite?"

"Not for this body," I said between a deep swallow of water and another smaller gag reflex.

She frowned. "I'm sorry."

"It's okay, I'll make something else," I said, and fed myself naan bread dipped in ranch sauce by my fresh arm for the rest of the evening. It twitched a bit worse than the rest, signals firing in a way it couldn't quite accommodate, but it was functional. It was my dominant arm, and, despite everything, it made me happy.

For the next year, it was the one part of my body left unchanged. Yes: three years now. Maybe this was what it was like to be inhuman.

I got another message from Katrine. It had two images. The first was a rejection for space travel—one-hundred-and-thirteen being a little too old—and the second was her strapped into a sim chair, goggles on her eyes and tube still jutting out of her throat. It had a pink scarf wrapped around it now.

...

When the fourth year hit, I'd officially made it longer in this body than the last one. I know, that bad. But it wasn't my fault that time. The twitches in that body had been almost minor, but combined with a bit of carelessness, a windy day, and a high bridge, they brought an end to the three-and-a-half-year-old body. I'd just really, really needed to be moving and the apartment was a closet in a shed in a building eighty stories high. No balcony.

I hit the water below the bridge hard, but titanium and carbon fiber and... I have no idea what we're made from anymore. But it's harder than skin. Harder than bone. Whatever it is, it *bends*. It *warps*. And it *bursts* through skin stretched tight like a drum.

I was found five hours later and told the body couldn't be saved as they ejected the chip and told someone, "He's not even good for scrap," and I pleaded through the agony no one had remembered to turn off that next time I would have what I wanted.

Eight weeks later I was in the new body and told it would be my last.

...

Technically, they could probably make us able to remember anything and everything. Make us more solid-state than brain tissue, but storage isn't that cheap, so they opted to let excess memories be pruned on top of losses. In my first few bodies, they could come and go at a sound, a smell, a touch. Resurface from years of disuse, covered in dust but nevertheless in stellar high definition, beat-for-beat remakes of experiences, never changing, never growing.

Those with the strongest emotional attachments got filed in front row directories, kept fresh like produce while those at the back, unincubated, unremarked, rotted away until they were overwritten with something of new insignificance.

Maybe *that's* why I've never been happy: happiness has always been a lukewarm experience, but pain has been something I was programmed to build and build and build. A distracted word from a friend turned into a burning indictment of my essence. How could happiness stand a chance against those odds?

It was fun when Rain would reminisce about the time we got food at that restaurant downtown—you know, the one with the black lights, all the food white and glowing neon?—and I couldn't scrounge up the name of the street. Or Damian talked about how much it had meant that one time I did—what was it he'd said, hell, I don't know—and the only memory I kept was of dirt, a tribute to my selfishness.

#

Five years.

Katrine, the bitch, was sending messages every other month now. "This should be the last time you hear from me," one message read. The signature at the bottom was appended with the caveat, "Dictated and not read." The next message, she asked me if I would like to come over for a visit, to say goodbye, though she was traveling again soon, so she understood if I didn't have time. I didn't, and by the time the next message greeted me she looked more like a corpse than ever— pictures showing eyes permanently shut—in a bubble under the sea.

There was still a chance, such a massive, *massive* chance that even when she died, she wouldn't win the lottery. About fifty Firsts died every two weeks and about a third of them put their bodies down for the lottery (according to my desperate Freedom of Information requests). So when she died I had, what, a one-in-seventeen chance?

I kept putting out more postings, but Katrine was the one and only person to respond in those five years.

It was as good as saying it was never going to happen.

On a particularly bad day, I went and got a brand new tattoo. My name in five big block letters across my chest (finally devoid of hair).

Elegant, but when I looked at it in the mirror, I cried and started wearing shirts to bed. Short sleeved, but only on the one side.

And then Katrine died.

The notification came in the middle of the night. A message two-hundred characters long and promising, "further communications" at its end. No pictures of Katrine were enclosed, just the words, "When you end up hating it too, try not to hate me."

It was a week and a half until the draw. A week and a half for other Firsts to die and dilute the odds. Never more had I wanted the promise of eternal life, if only for others.

#

I got into the habit of reading the obituaries for Firsts. They were tacked in front of the list of sequentials' two-sentence, nine-point tributes that nevertheless made the first two pages comprise just Aaa—Aad. The Firsts each got an entire page of gushing in twelve-point font.

I read about one man who, in his first two decades, had solved Pardu's Paradox. Dead after ninety-eight years and with a family waiting for him. I hated him.

I read about a woman who'd never done anything exceptional. "Loved by her friends and family," she kept her head down for eighty-eight years before passing away in her sleep, off to Venus for the next step in her journey. I hated her.

I read about a child who died. Sixteen, lacerated by a broken wire hanging loose in the city. Regretfully, she would not be joining her family. I felt sorry for her.

The final death toll for the two weeks came out to forty-seven, and I had no way of knowing how many had entered the lottery. But.

I. Got. The. Message.

This one was four hundred characters. It had my name and it had salutations and it had farewells and it had the words, "Please arrive at a medical center at your earliest convenience," couched in the most confused bureaucratic language I had ever read, as if they weren't sure they were really supposed to be following through on this last will-and-testament.

Neither was I.

"Do you… want us to come?" Rain asked.

"If you want. But. I don't know. It'll be fine, there won't be anything for you to do there."

She shrugged. "All right, I'll see you after?"

"Yeah, you'll see *me,*" I said, more than a little aware of how cheesy it sounded. Damian rolled his eyes. I laughed and waved goodbye with my good arm.

#

It was exactly as much of a mess as I expected when I arrived at the medical center. Somewhere downstairs, a body was put on hold for someone already inhabiting one—me. Somewhere else, Katrine's back-up drive had been crushed by a comically large shoe, unless her family had reneged on that part of the will.

Even as I sat outside the Outtake Technician's office, a heated voice could be heard debating a lawyer within. I should have brought a book. Instead, I inspected my good arm, turning over the hand, fingers flexing and clenching and covered in scars of the most benign kind from careless scrapes rather than a world's malicious intent.

The lawyer stalked out with a page covered in angry red pen clutched in his hand. I was kept waiting. And waiting. And waiting.

It felt like every day of the last five years bundled into a single anxious evening. People talking about me, but never to me. I thought about heading to the cafeteria for a snack, but the insane idea held me that if I left now, if they came for me and I wasn't there, if only for the briefest moment, it'd be all over. I'd miss my chance. I'd die encased in my last desperate attempt at autonomy, a name incongruously scratched across a well-muscled chest. I left just once for the bathroom and sprinted to and from it without washing my hands.

"Miss?"

I jumped, eyes snapping open. "Yes?"

The lawyer was back. He had a single page in his hand and motioned me inside the office.

"This will be your last, you understand?" I nodded. "A special exemption has been made, but it can't happen again." Again, I nodded. "Okay. Read this carefully, then sign. There." He pointed at the black box at the bottom.

My eyes skimmed. "In Accordance with... You hereby consent... Acknowledgement... Permit. Notwithstanding... Furthermore..." They were all the right words. I signed in a flourish with a signature I knew better than myself.

The technician was standing off to the side, looking moody. But once I was done, she said, "Okay. Let's go."

Every moment of those next thirty-three minutes and twenty-nine seconds can be replayed frame-by-frame in my mind. I could tell you the thread count of the technician's coat. The serial number of every piece of equipment I passed. Show you every moment the lights on the ceiling of the surgical room took an uncertain flush of power, hertz rising and falling. I could do the math to the eightieth significant figure for every minute I was there, if that's how sig figs work.

Then it was all simple. A brief plug into the base of my skull, creating a one-time backup. A thin needle was inserted below the eighth vertebrae and hit the kill-switch effortlessly.

I died.

...

On the other side I wasn't fuckable. I wasn't tall and slender. I wasn't wide-birthing hips and slight features. I was lopsided breasts with a feather-soft upper lip, slight hairs a touch on the dark side for skin that was a touch on the light. I could see where the wrinkles might form and where the tube would slot in below an Adam's apple that remained too pronounced.

But then again, the body, my body, worked. I looked in the mirror, vision permanently blurred at the edges. I said a name as if this twitching mass were mine.

...

Maybe there are three ways to get a new body. The first is to die: to take what you are given and deal with it. The second is to be so rich that discomfort is the name of a company you hold stock in.
The third is to say fuck it and reach to the wind. The third is to be lucky beyond belief and do something no one has ever done. The third is to do something no one will ever be able to do again.

The third is to give up being yourself to be—be—be—be—be—be—be—be—be—be—be—be—be—be—be—be—be—be—be—be—

THE GUILT MIRROR
Mickey J. Ellis

Pick up the phone. Look at your face reflected in the blackness of the screen. It's not easy to see yourself. But you know it's you. This dark reflection of yourself.

January 1ˢᵗ 2021

A reflection of a man

He looks back reflected in the mirror. A guilt mirror. The dust is thick. You can see the particles floating in the yellow light from the glowing bulb. Tiny particles made up of millions of smaller particles. This mirror hasn't been cleaned in almost a decade. He stares at you. A reflection. Not the real man. His hair is long and greasy. His pallid skin hangs off his face. He would be considered an ugly man. Objectively speaking. If you saw him walking towards you on the street you'd make an effort to avoid eye contact. You'd take out your phone and pretend to text and to swipe. To lose yourself in another world. A different reality. Another universe. An esoteric theory that enables observation to define what's real. Only when you look at this man does he become real to you. If you don't look at him he doesn't exist.

A photograph of a man

In this version of reality it was raining. It was probably only about two in the afternoon but it was so dark it seemed a lot later. Like five or six maybe. At the moment this photograph was taken the man was standing on the pavement by the wall just outside the graveyard. His clothes were drenched and his bad foot was throbbing. His head was foggy. In the background of the photograph there is another man. His mouth is open, yelling, shouting unheard words. The first man was tense, hearing the barrage of words. Uncomprehending but knowing what came next. The usual. That horrible moment when it feels like time is standing still. That few seconds when you know you're going to feel the impact of another person and there is nothing you can do about it. The humiliation and shock hitting hard as you crumple onto the floor. He had been hit more times than he could remember.

A photograph of a car
The screech of the tires broke that horrible tension. A red car. You can tell it is moving at speed. It came from nowhere as the man lurched across the road, determined to prove his alpha dominance on another, a grotesque man physically offensive in his inability to adhere to the accepted convention. He didn't see the car as he stepped onto the road. It didn't see him. Or certainly not until it was too late. The noise was grim. A big bang. A sickening crunch. A screech. And then a roar as the car drove off. You can see the man standing by the graveyard in the background. Frozen. It was still only about two in the afternoon.

I should leave this scene. But my phone is in my hand. I will just be a moment. Just a quick look to see what is going on in some other realities.

An image of a man
This guy's body is toned and ripples with muscles. He's a personal trainer. A man who spends his days in the gym, pushing people hard so they can achieve the picture perfect physique. A physique as picture perfect as the picture of him, life-size on the wall. He's a good guy. I mean he sometimes mutters things under his breath when

someone heaves and puffs to lift a weight. And if a girl waddles in with leggings that makes her arse look like cottage cheese he has to swallow down the bile of disgust that burns in his throat. In this photograph he stands tall, muscles bulging from under the straining fabric of his T-Shirt. He's taken the picture himself, pointing it in to the gym mirror. Post workout so his muscles are engorged and throbbing at their maximum. Evidence of his power. The sweat appears vivid on the marl grey fabric.

A photograph of a woman
You can see instantly how uncomfortable she looks in her brand new gym wear. Self-conscious. The label she forgot to take off in a rush in the changing rooms stabbing into her waist. Sweaty Betty. A school playground insult become an aspirational brand promising physical perfection. Although the Sweaty Bettys you see in the shop windows aren't like the sweaty bettys from school. They're lithe and beautiful. Not like this Betty. She's short. Pear shaped they call it. And coincidentally that was her name. Betty. You know it's her name because of the comment under the photograph. 'Specimen of the Day'. That's how her personal trainer began every post. His private profile obviously. 'Check out BETTY!! Thinks she can get fit! FAT STOOPID BTCH!!! LOL. He takes a photograph of every client on their first day of PT. He tells them it's so they have something to compare against when they get in shape. Before and after.

I don't judge. It's not my place.

A photograph of a coffee table
An empty tub of Ben and Jerry on its side, the sticky residue of Chocolate Fudge Brownie. Or Caramel Chew Chew. Or Chunky Monkey congealed onto an empty tube of Pringles. The sticky mess

dripping onto a Domino's pizza box. The sugary sweet liquidated trans-fat dribbling onto the photograph of a woman, wide-eyed and worried on the front of a brand new membership card.

A photograph of a woman
She's still wearing her gym clothes. Her arm is in mid-air. Caught in frame half way between its arc from bowl to mouth. Her eyes are puffy from crying. She heard what that bastard had whispered under his breath as she swung that kettle bell between her legs. Bent over and humiliated. In her other hand she holds a phone. She is staring purposefully at the screen. Eager to begin her nightly cathartic pastime. Pictures of people. Smiling. Tanned. Happy. Wealthy. Successful. Beautiful. Perfect lives. They knew what to show her. Knew how to really inspire her. Scrolling. Commenting.

A photograph of a man
Smiling proudly at the camera. Topless. Muscles bulging. Sweating.
Comment: sparklybetty9 Hope you get hit by a car and see how smug you look in a fucking wheelchair you CUNT.

A photograph of a girl
Pouting seductively at the camera. Kneeling on a bed. She's wearing a pink bikini. It leaves little to the imagination. Look closer. Pinch the screen and zoom into the worry across her glazed eyes.
Comment: sparklybetty9 Gang rape would be too good for that SLAG. GET AIDS AND DIE!!

I need to go home. I don't want anything to do with this. I read these comments and they hurt. I know their power. The wings of a butterfly and their unseen consequences.

A photograph of a room

In a different universe. A child's room. A room that cannot disguise the wealth and privilege that exists within its walls. You can just sense the room smells like roses. With a hint of mint. With a touch of lavender. On one wall there is a table covered in make-up. A mirror with light-bulbs all the way around like you'd see backstage at a glamorous West End show. Bottles and potions and creams and sprays. If you look closely you can see the words Fenty by Rhianna. If you zoom in to the photograph you can read the words Kylie Cosmetics. Scattered on the floor are various cuddly toys. A little green dinosaur. An old brown teddy bear with both eyes missing. A weird blue armadillo thing. A pink uni-kitty. Once precious. Recently cast aside. Thrown from the single bed in the corner. A bed dressed in a candy pink and blue stripe cover. You can tell the sheets are silk. The gravity is strong in this room. A quantum gravity that pulls its observer with an unexpected force. Observe that it is the room of a child. Observe that it is the room of an adult. It all depends on the perspective. On the bed side table are birthday cards. On the bed there's a pink bikini.

A photograph of a group

In this reality like so many others the rain continues to fall. A grey liquid filter that refracts light and distorts reality. The group are huddled in a bus shelter. Sheltering from the unending deluge. In the background you can see the light from the Shell garage. The photo cropped to hell. At the front of the photograph is a girl. Observed in one reality she is a child. In this reality she is an adult. She is holding a bottle of vodka in one hand, her arm held aloft. Her other hand raised in a 'V'. Her tongue sticking out in seductive defiance. She is in the middle of the picture. In the photograph there are five other people, all boys. You can see they are young but their posturing displays a menace at odds with their years. If you look closely you can see the worry in her eyes. If you really zoom into the photograph you can tell her eyes are rolling back in her head, rushing from the pill that her new boyfriend had just spiked her with. If you really look hard enough you can see the regret that she let her new boyfriend take those photographs of her this morning. That moment of observation when an infinite number of possible futures become a single irrefutable present.

The rain is falling in sheets now. Bouncing off the ground. The clouds create a claustrophobia. Making the world seem so small. Impossible to see anything beyond. I need to go home. But just one more look.

A photograph of a woman
Sitting on a couch. Her phone is on her lap and her shoulders are hunched. You can tell from the photograph that she's crying. Sobbing uncontrollably. He'd done it this time. 'Success'. Practice makes perfect. Death by two tonnes of metal. Not conventional but effective. He'd saved her life once. When she was on the receiving end of the abuse. He'd been there to reassure her that it was all going to be okay. That they weren't worth it. Sad little people hiding behind screens spewing their jealous bile. But they'd got him. A misjudged comment. A witch-hunt. The snowball effect of thousands of anonymous snowflakes. Woken up and taking offence on behalf of the hypothetical. She tried to push the image of the blood mixing with the rain water from her mind. His glazed eyes. Tried not to wonder which filter had been used. The one that really accentuated the contrast. She felt a tear run down her nose and watched it drop. She could make out her face reflected in the black screen.

I'm getting confused. I need to make sense of all this. There's too much noise. I don't know who these people are. Why are these photographs online? My vision is blurring with the sensory overload. The man is still lying in the road. Who is he? Is he the man from the photograph I saw? I try to scroll back to find it but it is lost. Replaced by new photographs. The bus-stop. There was a group of kids there but they've gone. Or is it a different bus-stop. Was that real or was it just a photograph? My reality is becoming blurred. I can hear a siren getting closer. I need to be at home. I need quiet.

A photograph of a woman

Caught in a moment. A split second. Her phone is held to her ear. Black kohled eyes wide in horror. Her other hand clenched into a fist. If you look closely you can see her white knuckles. This photograph has been taken at that very moment the news was processed by her brain. A billion synapses in perfect harmony. A billion synapses made up of a hundred trillion atoms. An unimaginably small event occurring in an incomprehensibly large universe. The tiniest spark of energy that causes a wave of incomparable emotion. In this universe. At this moment in time.

A photograph of a road

Taken from inside a car. The rain is falling hard. Bouncing off the windscreen. You can just about make out the road ahead. Just about make out the movement of other cars. Disorientating coloured blurs on the periphery of your vision. You can see a SatNav attached to the dashboard. If you zoom into the photograph you can just about make out the destination. You can almost read St Joseph's Hospital. You can just make out A & E Department. You can make out perfectly manicured nails painted Corail Colisee red. You can clearly see the Mercedes logo in the middle of the steering wheel. You can see a phone in one of her hands. If you pinch the screen you can make out some of the words on the text. You can read 'accident'. You can read 'hit by car'. You can make out 'I don't know!'

I feel like I recognise this woman. The car. It all seems so familiar. The photographs are gone as soon as I look at them though. I can't make any sense of this.

A photograph of a grey urban landscape
A rain-sodden street. A tenement building in the background. Grey and foreboding. You can see a bus-stop. A smashed vodka bottle. You don't notice what's happening in the picture at first. At first it seems innocent. Just a street like any other. Nothing out of the ordinary. You need to pinch the screen. Zoom in. Look really closely to see what's really happening in this photograph. You can just about make out a group of teenage boys at the entrance to the flats. They're huddled in a tight group. Dragging. Carrying. It's hard to see what's going on in the photograph. A blur of arms and legs. Mouths open, jeering.

I can hear a girl's screams. But I can't tell if it's in my mind or in the real world. The siren feels like it's on top of me now. All around. Inside my head. My clothes are drenched. The cold fabric burning my skin. The scream is getting louder. Am I screaming?

A photograph of a street
The photograph is taken from above. Perhaps from a fifth floor window of a block of flats. Perhaps from a girl's bedroom. Perhaps from the front room of a man living alone. It's hard to see clearly what is happening in the premature darkness. You can see a man on the other side of the street. You can tell his tracksuit is sodden. You just about see his discarded gym bag on the pavement a few metres behind him. You can tell he's running. Running into the street. His right arm thrown back as his left leg lunges forward. A prime specimen of a man. Fit and healthy. His mouth is open in a silent shout. It's impossible from the photograph to tell what he's saying. From the shape of his mouth it could have been 'Oi'. There's a possibility that it was maybe 'what the fuck are you doing?' The curl of his lips, the shape of his mouth it could have been 'leave her the fuck alone'. You can see a bus-stop. You can see a red car on the street. You can just make out the silhouette of a church steeple against the grey sky. You

can see a fat man. Holding his head. Pressing his hands into his ears. To block out the screams. To shut out the noise from the car engine. To stop the unending wail of the siren. Save his fractured senses from the bombardment of information overwhelming his mind.

A photograph of a car
Impossible to make out clearly. A blur of confusion. So much noise. A photograph where everything becomes indiscriminate. Subjective. A blur of green from a tree lined street. Or is it a rain drenched tracksuit top. A flash of red. A car. Or maybe lips. Screaming. Or maybe blood merging with rain. Black kohled eyes wide in horror. A smashed bottle of vodka. A pink dinosaur. An empty ice cream tub. An impossible blur of colour. Impossible to discern what is real. Whose reality you are observing. But if you really pinch the screen. Really zoom into the picture. There's only one thing in focus in all of this chaos.

A photograph of a man
He was clearly dead. The impact had thrown him forward and his head had hit the ground hard. His eyes were still open. I took my phone out of my pocket and opened Instagram. I had four different accounts. None of them real. Only the observation made these people real. Four people who didn't actually exist in your universe. Four different versions of reality. But even though they didn't exist, their gravity pulled you in ways not noticeable but palpably real. Dark matter. Negative energy. All the time I'd spent masquerading as a real person. A person of influence. Spinning reality to increase my gravity. Painstakingly, liking and following to maximise the dislike I could create. Attract and repel. I snapped a photograph. Filter. The rain and his blood merged nicely together. Post. His final moment frozen in time forever. It's what he would have wanted.

A reflection of a man
He looks back at himself, reflected in the blackness of the screen.

AN ESCALATION IN DIGRESSION

Nicholas E. Jung

April 29th 2020

Beginning

I doubt that you will find beneath these words, a story. Perhaps that is for the best. Our stories have become exhausted, their topography is all too similar. Stories exist to elicit an emotion; a firing of neurons and the associated elicitation of a physiological activity which acts as a Rorschach test dependent on how we lived our lives. Whether our parents beat us in the darkness of the attic, whether our first sexual experience was too fast etc etc etc. It seems best then to have our words return to their initial form. To act as echoes of the body's movement in space. Spoken softly against the ear of a loved one; tunneling through the external auditory canal, hitting the eardrum to send vibrations to push the oval window, to pass onto the cochlea in which reside tiny hairs who will reach out their keratin tips to hold the expressions of a day and change them into meaningful noise.

Middle

He walks onto the escalator and the escalator climbs. His feet are carried away with the accompanying feeling that his body is still. They had waited in line for hours, huddled under blankets to keep warm, breaking the rules of proximity out of necessity for survival. Now on the escalator the rules are being broken again. Cramped together, a mass of bodies intermingling into an indistinguishable single flesh. Proximity sheds many barriers; here it solidifies false individualism. He breathes slowly to control the inevitable rise in claustrophobic fear and his arm brushes against the woman beside him. She has dark hair, is 115lbs, 5'3", 32-25-34, 32DD meaning a calculated dress size of 4, shoe size 7, age of as writing 25. She reminds him of the actress in a pornographic film he had watched the other night while high[1] The escalator climbs parallel to the sheet of glass and steel that is the building's north wall. Outside there is the line of people waiting; a man and a woman stand together, fingers interlaced, staring straight ahead their eyes filled with erotic images of persons not present. The woman's makeup is heavy, blending her features into a contortion of white emptiness, *A Whiter Shade of Pale* would seem almost prophetic if

-----

1 More specifically he had watched *The Orifice* (a painfully obvious pun on the hit television show The Office starring Steve Carrell (US version) and Ricky Gervais (UK Version)) released 06/2014 from AVN Media Network. 236 mins; meaning 3.93333 hours of worship, not towards the heavens but downwards, towards the sexual organ a male uses to inseminate receptive mates during copulation. 3.93333 hours of intercourse that we, as readers might render mindless, meaningless. Without the want of procreation or the emotional connection of love, empathy, kindness…sexual intercourse transcends meaning and becomes nothingness into which the image is projected. The sex on the screen remains tantalizing only because there exists friction in a vacuum. To our character though a different understanding is gained. Under the influence of the psychoactive and hallucinogenic compound of 4-phosphoryloxy-N,N-dimethyltryptamine (colloquially psilocybin or magic mushrooms) (which is available from your local pharmacy for 9.99, as a treatment for depression and boredom), the video was as much a statement on 'our times' as Solzhenitsyn or Orwell were to theirs.

the warning signs of current fashion trends had not extended far into the 1500's.[2]

There is suddenly a short bang on the glass followed by a successive wave of tiny drum beats. The people in the line scatter as a flock of birds hits the glass, not realizing that transparency does not now equate to nothing. The glass remains beautifully intact, the birds do not. The force of the impact has broken their necks and caused them to fall on their backs. Most have died instantly but a few squirm legs and wings, trying to right themselves and return to the skies. Return to the forests and open air. Return to nowhere. The crowd quickly resumes its form, no one is shocked. The mass deaths of Aves - reports put the number anywhere from 100 million to 1 billion[3] - is as common now as the captivity of marsupials for exclusively 'selfie' use; slavery for reasons of cuteness and a trusting attitude.

The escalator climbs through the floors of the building, each one a mirror of the last. The entrance to the floor is a vestibule centrally adorned with a statue of a famous cartoon character blown up to twice the size one would expect, their physical characteristics exaggerated to the point of fetishization. The characters are all forged from polychromed aluminum and painted in bright colours to render an image that the artist must have consciously decided would be immortal. Popeye, Mickey Mouse, Homer Simpson, Bugs Bunny and others barely worth mentioning, for the reader can probably guess their identities, stare down at the shoppers; their gaze frozen in perfect

---

2 A reported recipe from the 17th century described a mixture of water, vinegar, and the use of white lead as a pigment. This, as you can imagine, caused lead poisoning, damage to the skin, hair loss and death. Today such cosmetics include hydroquinone and/or corticosteroids (for example hydrocortisone) and, in some cases, have been known to contain mercury.

3 Bird–building collisions in the United States: Estimates of annual mortality and species vulnerability *The Condor Ornithological Application The Condor*, Volume 116, Issue 1, 1 February 2014, Pages 8–23

judgment over the mortality of humankind. The remainder of the floor is a series of 9 shops hidden behind 9 identical wooden doors[4]. Consumers go from door to door, enter with nothing and exit with too much. Every floor is the same, they exist simply to be.

Interlude

4,173 words is a great deal and is something that requires an attention span missing from many readers right now. Flights by Olga Tokarczuk, written in what she calls a constellation style, first gave me the idea to write in vignettes as a way of overcoming this problem. Unlike her I will not add the pretence of connection…Next…I'd do this like a shot but unfortunately I'm too old…Next…I'm going to give you advice on the basics, and tips for advanced fiction writing; I'm going to encourage you on the difficult writing days and celebrate with you on the magical ones…Next…Today pianist Bruce Brubaker plays "The Poet Acts" from The Hours…Next…When a hamster eats better than you do…Next…Flash Sale: get 12 weeks for as little as $6. Plus, get a limited-edition tote…Next…This is Not A Drill is officially "Postponed"…Next…Celebrate 20 years of the International Space

---

4   There are 25 floors in this particular building; a modest size compared to the 95 floor *Peak Heights* in London and quite simply dwarfed by the 411 floor *SkySkraper* in Paris. Each floor as mentioned contains a central landing with 9 shopping experiences available. For the purpose of lessening consumer confusion all shops on all floors are identical. Although the facade of the building is constructed in the High-tech, Neo-Futurist, Proto-deconstructionalist architectural style of glass, concrete and steel; each floor is gaudily decorated in dark oak and white marble. This serves not only as a reflection of the more traditional roots of the building but is meant to illicit feelings of safety and luxury. The shops are as follows: Sears: Now For Lease (1), Victoria's Secret (2), McDonald's (3), Apple (4), Costco (5), True Religion Jeans (6), GAME (7), Supreme (8), Wells Fargo (9).

Station with this exclusive LEGO Ideas set...Next...It's World Art Day!

Here's some art I like...Next...Caption This...Next...Replace your notebooks and printed documents with the only tablet that feels like paper. Pre-order now to take advantage of our launch offer...Next... "I set out to look for dramatic scenes but ended up shooting mostly nothing at all." A photo essay of a city on pause: Next...Independent journalism needs your support...Next...Willie disapproves walks. Big time...Next...Go on a cosmic adventure through the pioneering space-race graphics of the former Soviet Union...Next...Someone doesn't approve of the rain keeping her from playing outside...Next... Why do we fall in love with one person and not another? This might explain it....Next...Arpin Philately has a large inventory of Canadian stamps, USA stamps, worldwide stamps, stamp albums and philatelic supply....Next...Month of inventory in the GTA tripled since the beginning of March 2020...Next...Lola says 'can you not!?!' I just can't resist that freshly groomed momo though...Next...Fine Italian style isn't going anywhere...Next...Bruce disapproves of his sister spying on him...Next...The perfect artwork for the kitchen. A lovely accessory that also helps you learn. Everything from sauce recipes, weights and measures, herbs and much more. Eco friendly and premium...Next...This Could Be You. Make yourself a Lord for as little as $49.95 today...Next...It's still sleep time according to 9 week old Gidget...Next...Brutal...Next...Tater Tot disapproves going to the vet for his vaccine appointment!...Next...Floating cities. Derelict desert kingdoms. Submerged ocean civilizations.

Don't miss this kit's timeless textures, organic shapes and fluid structures!...Next...Heartbreaking...Next...What if the US would not have joined WW1? Simulate any WW1 scenario you can think of!...Next...Please. Go. Away...Next...For 48 Hours, 2-Piece Suits starting at $49....Next...This is how over 10,000 people are crushing their fitness goal right now. The Hadrian's Wall, a 90 miles Virtual Challenge that takes you along the historic Hadrian's Wall path across the north of England…Next…The geopolitical consequences of the pandemic will be long-lasting—and unfortunate. Some fear China will be the winner…Next…Ever since King Karl IX of Sweden founded Skultuna in 1607, we have been dedicated to manufacturing the antiques of tomorrow. Wear them, love them, pass them on to the next generation. Free Home delivery World Wide & free gift wrapping…Next…I read an article the other day which claimed that the internet has made us creatures of immediacy, we respond to that which is directly in front of us and ignore all other happenings which, while still occurring, now occur in the periphery[5]…Next…"Take a

———

5 Object Permanence is the term which describes a person's ability to know that an object continues to exist even when said object cannot be seen. Despite much study being done regarding the psychological phenomenon of object permanence, and the important influence that object permanence has on a person's intellectual, sensory and ego development, little is known regarding the origins of the phenomenon. In Piaget's classical theory, object permanence was thought to be a developmental achievement because infants progressed from initial failures to successful search for hidden objects (*New findings on object permanence: A developmental difference between two types of occlusion*; Moore & Meltzoff, 2014. British Journal of Developmental Psychology").

Opposing classical theories sits Lacanian postmetademodernism which argues that the post-semantic meta-realism of Descartes intuitively leads to object permanence being the acceptance of the *Inner Ghost*, as opposed by Gildert Ryle, in an attempt to resurrect the egotistic notion of pre-Hegelian dialectic reasoning. The absurdist view that a child might understand the continued existence of an object outside the reach of sensory mechanoreceptors, leads to an acceptance of the neocolonial post feminist view that objects outside our vision continue to hold the stability of the Schrödinger equation $i\hbar\frac{\partial}{\partial t}|\psi(t)\rangle = \hat{H}|\psi(t)\rangle$. This in turn leads to a rejection of Hilbert's 'non-joyful' space and an acceptance of the proto-Kondo 'clean vision' of quantum mechanics suppressed by the assumption that all wave functions are normalized. We are left with a non-relativistic quantum mechanics, seat", such is the motto of this auction exclusively dedicated to seats. Baroque, Rococo, Modern, Neo-Classical, Art Nouveau, Louis XV

———

the probability current $\mathbf{j}$ of the wave function in one dimension, defined as $j = \frac{\hbar}{2mi}\left(\Psi^* \frac{\partial \Psi}{\partial x} - \Psi \frac{\partial \Psi^*}{\partial x}\right)$, , therefore a collapse of the wave function, Einsteinian relativity and a child unable to play peek a boo. This hysterical science is certainly better explained by the Brother's Grimm in the following way:

"There once was a girl with no object permanence so that every time her eyes were covered the world no longer existed. This scared the little girl and she did everything she could to keep her eyes open. She tried to make sure that nothing ever covered her eyes, which worked sometimes, but she quickly found that her body fought against her and would always win. It kept making her shut her eyes and the moment that happened the world would disappear. Blinking was the worst and it happened, to her count, 15 times every minute! She tried not blinking and would hold her eyes open for as long as she could, but eventually her eyes would sting so badly that she would have to shut them. Sleeping was another problem the little girl had. Everyday around 9 o'clock her eyes would feel very heavy and she would run; scared of the disappearing world.

One day the little girl had a brilliant idea she would just tape her eyes open. She found some tape and tried to do just that but the tape was not strong enough and when 9 o'clock came, her eyelids shut. The next idea the little girl had was to pry her eyes open with matchsticks. She took 6 sticks and forced them in the eye socket. They worked a little better and the little girl was able to keep her eyes open till 11 o'clock but eventually the matchsticks broke under the pressure and sent splinters into her eye. She decided that she wouldn't do that again. The little girl then decided that the best option was to sew her eyes open with a needle and thread. We will spare the reader the unpleasant details of this debacle but needless to say that plan didn't work and you'd think the stupid little fucker would have gotten it by now" (*Children's and Household Tales, originally entitled Kinder- und Hausmärchen.* Jakob and Wilhelm Grimm, 1812-1858).

period, from different continents, choose your favourite chair!... The article argued that this mental phenomenon did not begin with the advent of the internet, but it seems that the advancements in communication technology have enhanced our pre-diminished ability to acknowledge that which we cannot see...Next...It's no secret that I have an obsession with Scandinavian culture. Today I'm celebrating earth day with a look back at my time in Norway, one of the most beautiful countries I have ever visited. Norway offers a culture and landscape like nothing I have ever seen and I truly cannot wait to go back...Next...Much of the problem comes from how people act on social media. The typical criticisms against social media is that due to the amount of information present people tend to only look at things which align with their own views. Algorithms then force us to only see things which correspond to what we were seeing before, essentially erasing the Other...Next...We're waiting to be safe. Waiting for hugs, high-fives and freedom to play...Next...Of course this view is an oversimplification of how the internet and social media are actually used. Individuals do not search for things they agree with or show who they actually are. Instead they create for themselves a persona of who someone else wants them to be. We only share, good or bad, that which will positively enhance our social image...Next... Never forget your Skin Elixir. Just cause we're in quarantine doesn't mean we can't have nice Hair, Skin & Nails...Next...In this way the content of our echo chambers is dictated by our friends[6]. Who we are

------

6 By grouping all people (friends we haven't seen in years, family members distant or otherwise, ex-girlfriends and boyfriends, actual real-world friends, virtual friends) under the same blanket term of 'Friend' we degrade the term. We ignore the real-world experiences that leads us to declare someone as our friend and conflate the experience of the virtual with the actual. Can virtual experiences be valuable? Of course, but they also have the propensity to be false and misleading, with people who exist simply as an image rather than a person in all their elegant complexity.

is a mimicry of their desire...Next...I disapproved of that already!...
Next...I've probably lost your attention as a reader by now, feel free
to click away...Next...Explore the history of European painting in
the unique context of a Christie's Old Masters sale, with a virtual
preview...Next...She has a case of the Mondays...Next...Inclusion
Criteria and Definition of Fatality...Next...Next...Next...Next.

Beginning of the End

We are back in the building observing, after a long breath of fresh
air (something not available to those inside), and see our character,
standing still, as the escalator climbs. He is nearing the end of his
journey and, as is often the case with travellers, he looks behind him to
see his progress. The beginning cannot be seen. There are thousands
on the escalator, crammed and cramped, their faces obscuring his
view. The faces are different and yet the same, a carbon copy of the
original form carved by different artists who with them, bring their
own interpretation. He remembers stories of when humanity used to
believe that a single being (a "God" he recalls, although there were so
many names) had forged everything. That myth had been eradicated
through an understanding of biology and physics but, perhaps, hidden
under the mountain of information that had been acquired, there
had been a loss of understanding of the unknowable and with it, an
understanding of true progress. The technological advances that he
lived with were remarkable, even to those that live within them but
each step forward is accompanied by a step towards demise. The
invention of the boat is simultaneously the invention of the shipwreck.

He allows himself to slip into the realm of fantasy. A beach with
sparkling blue water, pale white sand and a cloudless sky. A jagged

cliff on which sits rows of white houses and contrasting azure roofs[7]. Away from the city, away from the crowds.

He is brought back to reality with the sharp reminder that where there are houses there are people and where there are people there are inevitably crowds. He wants to be alone. Even his fantasy betrays the truth that 'to be alone' is a condition of the past, whereas loneliness is a very present feeling.

He can hear the announcements. The speakers ceased playing classical music three floors ago, no longer needing to lull people into the building, and they now spit out obscene pornographic descriptions of the type of people who buy a certain raincoat or a certain suit, preparing them unconsciously for the act of purchasing. Most of the people on the escalator are return customers and have heard this spiel before; as such they begin to look out the windows and long to be out of the building's embrace. The weather has turned nasty since the beginning of his journey and he realizes that a storm is definitely coming. The clouds are black and he can feel the pressure of the climate pushing the air from his lungs. He can feel the beginning of a headache and salivates at the thought of buying a valium. The sound of the speakers does not help.

There are bright fluorescent screens surrounding the escalator now, advertising the many recreational activities one can partake in. They are bright and flashy, blaring images in colours that he would not have thought were possible. The resolution is amazing, too realistic and he begins to feel the uncanny feeling that the screens are

---

7 During the The Greek junta, also known as the Regime of the Colonels, it became a legal requirement for Greek houses to be painted blue and white. This means that the iconic white houses are symbols of military dictatorship and authoritarian control. Such information is readily available yet we still maintain that these houses are beautiful symbols of island paradise. I assume the reason for this collective amnesia is that the truth is not quite as tourist friendly.

not screens at all, rather they are windows into which consumers are invited to gaze into the lives of what they could have. He had once participated in a recreational activity, a game called three card monte[8] which involved choosing the red queen from three different face down cards. He had lost all his money before being able to make any of his purchases and thus his social standing had fallen. The screens do not help his headache.

In the Belly of the Whale

When I look in the mirror I see a man, in his mid-twenties, suffering, in all likelihood from androgenic alopecia (a condition I try to maintain through a regimen of testosterone inhibitors). I am slim and have only recently put on weight. Consequently, when I raise my arms above my head, my rib cage is still prominently displayed. I see that my skin is dry, the area between the eye brows is flaking. My nose has a number

––––––

8 A fun little exercise related to three card monte, consider the following situation: Walking in Hyde Park a statistician encounters a person playing three card monte. She knows that statistically the red card is almost always the first on the right and flush with cash she decides to play. She bets £100. The cards are shown, flipped over and shuffled around. As she is about to choose, a stranger comes up and says that the card in the middle is the red card. Which card should she pick? In this example, the statistician might hesitate and should seriously entertain the possibility that the red card is in the middle and, while she should not be condemned for picking the card in the middle, it is not the one she *should* pick. Why?

Answer: I believe that in this case the statistician, at the risk of looking foolish, should pick the first card on the right as this is the one that she has the most reason to believe will be the correct card.

of small blackheads that I have tried, since my early teens, to dispel through the use of devices and face cleaners.[9]

My teeth are fairly white, slightly coloured from too much coffee, but all present and accounted for. The bottom row of teeth seem sharper than would be normal and are out of perfect alignment. This is something that does not bother me as much as it once did. I am not a fan of my nose, I think it is far too large, but my eyes I do like. They change colour and, I have been told, are kind (although whether ascribing anthropomorphic traits to eyes displays great intellectual ability or profound ridiculousness remains to be seen).

I describe myself not in order to gain sympathy but rather to make me real. All living things boil down to the images they are, the stronger the image, the more existent the thing. Yet the image of an author is normally hidden from the viewer. Their image is a mirror of the reader's own imperfections, their own self. In some ways I believe that the portrait of the artist is a more exact image of the reader than that they see in the mirror.

End

He is still on the step waiting, as the escalator climbs into the embrace of the mall, letting his mind run into the dark recesses dug by the microchips. He doesn't need to do this, he does not need to wait. Nothing here needs to be bought but he will nonetheless pull out his card, like a thin plastic phallus. He will buy and buy and buy; risk his life and expose himself to the bacteria and viruses, the pollutants[10]

---

9   Blackhead Remover Pore Vacuum Cleaner - LONOVE Upgraded Blackhead Vacuum Rechargeable Face Vacuum Come done Extractor Tool for Blackhead Whitehead Acne Removal, 5 Adjustable Suction Power and 4 Probes and Seaweed Deep Cleansing Gel Face Wash.

10 Common pollutants include: ozone, Carbon Monoxide, Sulfur Dioxide, Lead, Nitrogen Oxides, Particle Pollution (examples include: nitrates,

not out of need but because he, like you and I, need to fill the empty spaces. The girl whose arm he brushed against earlier looks down at the previous floor to where police officers are arresting a man, evidently for shoplifting. She turns to him and rolls her eyes. He smiles back at her and feels the need to grab her by the shoulders and kiss her. He wants to hold her tightly and whisper in her ear that everything is going to be okay, that the world can change, that people are strong and fundamentally good at heart. He wants to take her by the hand, this girl from the psilocybin induced night, and run down the escalator, run out the door, run away; like the birds, to the natural forests. But the moment the thought is finished it is replaced by the friendly jingle of the escalator. He has arrived at floor 25. He runs through his purchasing list in his head again and mentally adds oranges to it.

---

organic chemicals, soil, metals, sulfates, and dust particles), Carbon Dioxide, Methane, Chlorofluorocarbons. Common bacteria include: Escherichia Coli, Campylobacter Jejuni, Salmonella, Legionella Pneumophila, Cryptosporidium Staphylococcus aureus, Chlamydia Trachomatis. Common viruses include:, Herpes Simplex, Rhinovirus, Bronchitis, Gastroenteritis, Human parainfluenza virus, Respiratory syncytial virus.

IN ORDER NOT TO SLEEP
U.H Dematagoda

'Prolonged periods of self-correction rarely become bulls', Monday 12 August 23:25, Flight BA 178 to LDN Heathrow – *Boarding* – C17. 'The forthcoming implementation of reforms now well progressed, though this has taken longer than anticipated and originally intended due to the scale and complexities of the reforms proposed, and the projected effects on the largest markets. Meaningful progress has been made to mitigate systemic risk, specifically central clearing – and to a lesser extent credit default swaps – will lead to simplification and greater resilience'. Notes: 7004.10, +41.12, +0.59%, 11307.12, +115.49, +1.03% *und so weiter*…Courtney, 26, Brooklyn, NY; Erin, 29, Manhattan, NY; Chloe, 23, Bedford-Stuyvesant, Brooklyn, NY; Abigail, 26, NY, NY… "Hey" – "So what are you doing over here?" "Sorry, on a flight back to London now…coming back next month"… maybe I can make your legs shake then. Hehe what a Creep. "Ok maybe see you then xxx". *Hallo Mama, ich bin schon im Flugzeug. Ich rufe dich morgen früh an.* 'It's been a great year in light of the obvious fact that, when you look at the prevailing sentiment at the beginning of the year, it's completely surpassed the most bullish predictions. It's the type of year which one wants to really take some time to appreciate – there's been a nice cumulative wealth effect warming most portfolios across the spectrum. Self-corrections rarely becomes bulls, but I'm tempted to stick my neck out and say that it's pretty certain to be one by the close of the year'. "Sir, we're taking off." Flight Mode. Note:

The model presented is estimated in light of maximum likelihood – and the estimated results are given in figures 1 to 3. In panels 1, (a), (b) and panel 2 present the conditional numeric gaps associated with OTC market and the wide variances between the 5th and 95th quantiles. As can be observed, the left distribution is skewed, reflecting the deterioration of conditions and the palpable volatility witnessed in the first and second quarters. Nevertheless the ultimate distribution is conditionally Gaussian. In light of the velocity capacity provided by our infrastructure in the CME, we are likely to see optimal conditions for maximum return soon. 'Larissa, I'm sorry but I can't seem to stop thinking about you – and how we left things between us, it doesn't seem right to me that we should be apart now when we were so happy together before, even if it seems now like such a short time…I haven't been sleeping much without you lying next to me – even those three or four hours don't seem worth it, if I can't wake up next to you. Please write back to me.' "Water please. And a whiskey." "What kind?" "It doesn't matter."

Primary:ataxia, cognitive dysfunction, constipation, depression, difficulty in micturition, drowsiness, dysarthria, fatigue, memory impairment, menstrual disease, nervousness, sedated state, skin rash, tremor, weight gain, weight loss, anxiety, blurred vision, diarrhoea, insomnia, decreased libido. Other:depersonalization, hyperventilation, hypoesthesia, hypotension, paresthesia, sexual disorder, sialorrhea, muscle twitching, and increased libido.

Seldom have you understood me, rarely have I understood you. Battery 15%. Plugged in, charging. *In the classroom, empty of tables and chairs – Hannes was there; the teacher an amalgamation of several unpleasant bureaucratic faces, one of which is the sour-faced receptionist in the airport lounge and the other a man's, none too distinct but no less cloyingly familiar and another girl, Becky 24, Greenpoint, Brooklyn, NY, and another, perhaps Morgan, 28, Bushwick, NY - all these faces coalesce into a mess of upturned noses, vacant cybernetically tuned eyes, plump lips and furrowed brows, the teacher has set me a task that relates to the upper part of my own body, the neck, the throat and the contents of the skull, which*

I see before me as though on the dissecting table, yet I don't seem at all cognisant of their absence and feel little distress nor horror – I soon grow bored of this task, however, and I recall the work of that great contemporary philosopher of pessimism, who held sway in the classroom over his adoring students, whom he would then follow to the bars and ply with alcohol in the hopes of fucking them; he had hope, it's true... The phone vibrates with the weight of 57 unread emails and an alert for a category 3 storm which is projected to hit the Eastern Seaboard – I leave the Westphalian classroom and go outside to hail a London cab to take me through another magic roundabout, the words of my actual father ringing in my ears in all of their stagnant mediocrity. There's little significance to this disorder. Note: Bulls often become Bears, and so on. Battery Full. Tuesday 12 August 5:03 am, Flight BA 178, baggage reclaim 6. Holly, 26, Islington, Kamala, 25, Leytonstone, Keisha, 29, Hounslow. *Bist du gut angekommen? – Ja, ich rufe dich später an.* 'Larissa, just ignore that other text – sorry for being weird.'

"Bermondsey, mate."

"Been anywhere nice?"

"Just work."

"You look knackered mate."

"Never really slept."

Note: The jurisdictions under consideration have continued to make significant progress in implementing reforms to regulatory frameworks to promote the non-centralised clearing of standardised OTC derivatives, and to improve the level of risk associated, yet there remains significant political resistance to implementing all recommended changes. I am afraid that, despite the progress made in the intervening years, the events of 2010 have made regulatory authorities overly cautious about the potential offered by emergent technology. It is unclear how to approach this potential bottleneck, nor what the long-term strategic implications will be. Fabienne, 32, Southwark. 'Late night or early morning? Xxx.' 'Both.' "Where shall I drop you off?" "Here. But I'm coming back out...30 minutes, tops." An impressive architecturally designed abode, with an abundance of natural light along with a sleek contemporary interior. The accommodation comprises a large entrance hall with storage, and impressive reception room with exposed cast iron beams and wood flooring, which opens out onto a terrace providing stunning City views, stylish open plan fitted kitchen with stone work tops, integrated appliances and a breakfast bar, master bedroom One with en-suite shower room, double guest bedroom Two, and a family bathroom. The now empty apartment is suffused with an odour of stale newness, perfectly ordered yet lacking vitality. I peel off my yellowed shirt, moistened to the skin of my back – pull down my trousers and pungent boxer shorts, and climb into the shower. Note: under the internationally agreed timetable for the aforementioned reforms, the end of the coming week is the deadline for the implementation of comprehensive margin requirements; 4 out of the 5 jurisdictions under consideration are projected to meet this deadline, with the prospect of this happening in the 5th now uncertain due to recent political turbulence, the collapse of the coalition government and the prospect of a change in leadership. Depending on the resolution of these variables, it is optimistically expected that jurisdiction 5 may complete implementation by the end of the current quarter. This presents both opportunity and potential volatility, which require action or mitigation respectively. The water descended forcefully onto the marble floor of the shower and pummelled the sides of the glass cabinet as voices escaped from the speaker in the bedroom, seeping in through the open shower room door. 'We're joined on this week's show by the author of *Persistence*, a ground-breaking and youthful work of considerable merit, unashamedly self-regarding and confessional - but possessing a great deal of humour, it focuses on the relationship between two female friends from university through graduation, and their encounters with the uncomfortable realities of contemporary life and love – it is transgressive, and filled with radical honesty and beauty. The novel recounts the bourgeoning sex....' The voices became more and more indistinct, dissolving as they merged with the tranquilizing ambience of the shower until they resembled nothing more than a low level hum of recondite noise, of facile affirmation and polite contention. I feel a powerful stream of warm water crashing at my temples, dripping down my back and legs onto the floor where the sinkhole is blocked by clumps of brown hair – and the sunken rectangle in which I stood fills with water, steadily rising up until it comes to the top of my ankles. I close my eyes. Only a few dreary particles of purple spectral light danced across the stage and illuminated the all too brief darkness. Too many thoughts occurred inside my desiccated brain, overfull and bursting through its weakly sewed seams – but among them was one, that of Larissa. I stared at the tap handle, a glob of white viscous shampoo hung precariously at the edge of the handle – I kept staring for some time, wishing to wipe it off but somehow incapable of doing so. The stream of water coughed and spluttered and suddenly became cold, but I couldn't move…finally I managed to reach towards the tap, but the muscles snapped my arm back to its original place at my side. The water grows colder but I've become immobile, the tranquil warmth steadily replaced by a foreboding chill. I exhale deeply, reach out my arm out and switch off the shower, climbing out of the warm soapy puddle. My gums bleed as I brushed my teeth. A bitter copper taste filled my mouth as it mixed with the sharp mouthwash, which I spit out after ten seconds, filling the sink with a sticky stream of brownish green froth. Drying myself off with a towel in the bedroom, I put on a clean light blue shirt, a dark blue wool checked suit and a black knitted tie. The car was waiting as I emerged from the apartment. I climb silently inside and the door shut with a pathetic click. From outside the window, I sense the rancid yellow darkness beginning to transmute into a more unforgiving cold blue, as the car pulled off the kerb and drove towards the city.

"Alright Fritz? This is the new intern: Ella."

"Emma."

"Emma. Right, whatever. Anyway, she's available."

"Available for what?"

"Fuck sake mate…I dunno. Just take her off my hands for two hours would you mate – she's supposed to be shadowing me or something, I don't fucking know. How was New York then?"

"Fine. Listen, I don't have time for this – take her somewhere else."

"Do me a solid mate, I'll owe you. Cheers Fritz, I gotta go to the dentist mate."

"Bullshit."

"Your name's Fritz?"

"No."

"Then why does he call you that?"

"My mum's German, I was born there."

"Right, because you don't have an accent."

"Dulwich."

"Oh right, where'd you go to uni then?"

"Listen, Emma. I have to submit a report in an hour…so can you occupy yourself with something while I get on with it?"

"Of course, no worries."

"Thanks."

Note: Mitigation requires consideration and careful consultation with our various stakeholders in Jurisdiction 5, however it is more than likely that regulatory authorities are already in dialogue with these with respect to the ways in which they intend to enact proposals, and how not doing so may detrimentally effect their mandates. We must acknowledge from the outset that regulatory authorities are primarily concerned from an internal market integrity perspective, and as a rule do not compile transactional data made by foreign subsidiaries. The political situation is likely to magnify this, however we recommend our subsidiaries to exercise caution. 'Reports of a potential terror incident around Clapham junction, no fatalities, suspect apprehended. Police advise Londoners to stay away from the area as operations are ongoing.' Becky, 24, Hackney Wick, London…Text: 'One down for fives, Bethnal Green, 7pm – you in?' 'I've gotta work.'

"How are you doing, are you alright? Do you have a minute?"

"Sure."

"Come and sit down. I read your draft."

"Is there the problem?"

"There won't be a problem, because I've pushed the presentation forward to Thursday morning."

"But what exactly is the problem?"

"There won't be a problem."

"Ok, but is there room for improvement?"

"This isn't a zero sum game, despite its appearance – it's important to keep this in mind."

"I don't follow."

'You don't follow because you're trying to get ahead of yourself. It's important to take a step back and survey the terrain, if only occasionally.'

"There isn't time. It's time sensitive."

"It's important to make time…just indulge me a little. The problem with your generation is impatience, and I think this is amply reflected."

"But this doesn't give me anything to go on…"

"There is a bigger picture, despite the pervasive atomisation – I think you sense this as well. What I need from you is to take a step back, and reassess your recommendations. This has the potential to be a formative moment."

"The last time was supposed to be the same."

"It's an accumulation of moments, but this one in particular will be decisive…for you. Just remember: blue oceans. Blue oceans still exist in abundance, they're out there – just waiting to be discovered. The uncontested, the untrammelled."

'But I'm unsure…I'm unsure if this is the case.'

"You need to become convinced of it…because as it stands, what you've provided isn't fit for purpose. Thursday then?"

Catalina, 30, Leytonstone, London. 'Hello handsome, do you want party with me?' Note: 7004.10, +41.12, +0.59%, 11307.12, +115.49, +1.03% *zum Beispiel.*

As the day wore down into night once more, I stood up from my desk, removed my ear buds and stared down at the rows of backlit rectangles, now mostly free of people and commotion, but still flickering with varied-coloured sparks of data pulsating across the screens – in previous years the rows were immense, stretching the length of the floor, onto other floors and other buildings, but recently the screens had started to disappear; at first it had been gradual, but then more rapidly, with the unplugging and removals now a daily occurrence, more and more people began to wander around aimlessly among these rows, perhaps oblivious to the fact that their function was becoming more and more superfluous and decorative. Information had ceased to flow to the centre from across oceans and rivers, under streets and up wires, flowing inexorably to towards these screens; instead it has begun to branch outwards to the peripheries, it had taken flight, in airborne waves cascading through the skies, outwards to warehouses populated by more substantial machines ceaselessly blinking and transmitting, never sleeping.

"Come on Fritz, we're heading down to *The Hippogriff* for a couple."
"I've got to work."
"Come on, just for a couple – rounded up the interns, we're gonna show them what really goes on here."
"No, sorry."
"You're coming…come. Not leaving till you fucking come."
"Fine, just for a couple."

...

"Fritz, go and order a bottle of Borolo – this wine's shit."

"Wait a second…"

"Put your phone away mate, have a drink."

"I'm just sending an email."

"Gimme that, you twat. Here Ella, hold onto this for me."

"It's Emma?"

"Yeah whatever…what did you study then?"

"Italian and theatre."

"Sounds shit…what kind of theatre?"

"Mostly physical and contemporary…I'm interested in women's bodies?"

"Aren't we all."

"But I'm interested in their different forms, and the ways in which they take up space?"

"But you're quite svelte, innit. You don't really take up that much space at all….'

"Erm…I don't think you understand?"

"Birds don't take up a lot of space…unless they're fat munters. But whatever. If I give you five hundred quid, would you snog Rachel here?"

"Erm, Fuck off?"

"Oh, she'll go far! Fritz, go get another bottle for fuck sake."

"I'll join you."

"Where did you go to Uni, then?"

"Birmingham"

"Oh, right….what did you study?"

"Philosophy."

"What, like Derrida and all that?"

"Like modal logical and analytic."

"Cool…you know, I don't think I'll be coming in after tomorrow."

"How come?"

"It's really not for me…they had to twist my arm to go in for this, it was set-up, you know, but it's not really my thing?"

"I see. Have you been to Italy a lot?"

"Yeah…loads. I've been going since I was little. My parents have a house there, near Lake Garda."

"So…you've been to Gabriel D'Annunzio's monument to Italian Victories?"

"Is that the weird house with the warship in the garden? Yeah, I went once."

"You've seen the Puglia? I'm curious, what was the sensation you received – when standing atop that magnificent structure, which appears as if frozen at the very point of its launching – forcing itself upon the supplicant virginal landscape, and menacing the placid water below. Did you not feel a sensation of immense power and invincibility?"

"You're kind of weird, aren't you?"

"I suppose I am."

"No worries, I'm a little weird too! But yeah…not really, I was there with my boyfriend – well ex-boyfriend now - and it was raining most of the time? But I remember we met this cute old couple from Croatia, they only spoke a little Italian – I think they were from some place called Ustasi? They were so cute though.'

"Right. I think I should head back to the office."

"It's almost 3am? You should probably go to bed? Can we share a cab?"

…

With a casual "I don't usually do this", she was already in the midst of undressing, jettisoning any semblance of decorum as the front door closed. Note: the ragged natural contours and imperfections of female flesh are hideously exacerbated by this bedroom light, which was intended to be soft, but is instead almost too much like the daylight it purports to compensate. Needless to say, it must be replaced. In any case it was already Wednesday 13th of August, 4am (NYSE 20:30, SEE, 8:30, JPX 10:30), and my thoughts turned once more to mitigation strategies. Jurisdiction 5…"Why are you just standing there?" "I want to watch you play with yourself first." She complies. Note: it may be much harder to comply with the regulatory authorities in Jurisdiction…Before long I found myself confronted by a darkness, like that of some primordial cave, damp and hungry – something pink, delicate and raw concealed in its depths, a mortal wound, as unredeemable as nature, once spurned, and now advancing in wrath. I wanted more than anything to avert my eyes, but found that I was incapable - deprived of its illusion of control, my mind began to race to all those places which had for so long remained in place, but had lain dormant. The world was once more becoming enchanted. I felt myself recoiling in horror from her chaotic moans. "You look as if you want to eat me up." "Not yet." "Well…do you mind if I use my toy?" "I don't have any toys…" "I have one in my bag." She giggled "…I kinda knew I'd get bored at work today" A rapid and resonant hum broke the spell, as she manoeuvred the device with a deft hand to all the places where it was required…the scene began to stabilise, her breathing steadied and her moaning fell into line with the pulsations, cauterising the wound - so that it may heal. My distress lessened. She reached a muted and desultory climax, and began to look forlorn. She looked down at my flaccid cock.

"I guess this isn't going to happen, is it?" She asked, looking me over, after some moments.

"I'm sorry, I don't think I can."

"Ok…no worries. So how long have you lived here for? It's a big place for one person."

"About three years."

"Do you want me to leave?"

"Do you want to stay?"

She leaves. 6am. 'Hot teen sister creampied in hotel room.' 'Son fucking stepmom.' 'Stepbrother and stepsister fucking in bedroom.' 'FFM with mom and stepsister.' 'Mom teaches me how to fuck.' Note: there appears to be an emergent pornographic trend related to the absence of what was once described as the 'fundamental signifier.' There is of course some significance to this. If we are to ascribe a value to these developments in terms of their relative transgressive quality, against their putative erotic value (minimal) – the resultant distribution would be…degenerate. No pun intended. I'm finding it difficult to complete with what is being offered up here. I allow my thoughts drift. Larissa liked me to choke her when I was fucking her from behind, but I always felt that this was a concession as opposed to a genuine desire on her part – but I wasn't really into it, so what was the point? Moot point. The point is…the point is…*women prefer to be devoured whole, there's no sense in nibbling around the edges. Angela, 29, Walthamstow – perhaps she knows exactly what I'm talking about. She has that sublime quality behind the eyes which make all other women look upon her with contempt, but clearly she isn't overly bright – and in fact doesn't really need to be, but we'll humour her nonetheless. A physician as well? Brains and beauty! And like most women of her genre, she naturally veers to the right…though you'd never notice on first glance, or upon listening to her faux compassionate entreaties. Absolutely nothing radical about honesty. You're a fool if you think so. Generally speaking men have no conception of happiness in its totality, aside from the sum obtained by the accumulation of a variety of more or less minor pleasures, which grow more ephemeral and miniscule by the day. It is necessary to take a position prior to any form of assembling and ordering – that is the point at which the encounter will take place. Out of the nothingness, which preceded any form of Reason or End (Telos?) Nothing is the origin of the world, and the ultimate sum of all of these accumulations will amount to nothing…streams falling parallel to each other within a void…but this is no reason to despair…because out of this nothingness something will take hold…as it has always taken hold…the swerve will come eventually, the collision is inevitable, and we know not what it will bring. As an afterthought: women know exactly what happiness is, and more importantly, know how it's defined and quantified, both temporally and qualitatively. Give her a bag of happiness, a pitcher*

of happiness: half a pound of happiness! But only for a specified amount of time…
There's probably a book called 'How to get Enough Happiness' or some shit. And
it's probably written by a woman lol! Nom du Pére, Nom du Pére! Nom Nom Nom.
Devour them whole! Mein Vater! Warum hast du Angst? 7am. Alarm.

To: Larissa Licht <larissa_91@________ >
Wednesday, 08:30, 14th of August

Dear Larissa,

This email is quite difficult for me to write because I find that I am
incapable of summoning up the appropriate emotions to express.
Indeed, at present I feel that I'm unable to define, with any degree of
certainty, exactly what type of sentiment is appropriate. Contrition?
But I feel no contrition at all. Nor do I feel particularly despondent. In
truth, the emotions which I felt after you had left can be attributed to
an injunction, a mandate from some spectral authority that deemed
them appropriate to the occasion. I was thus compelled to act as
if your departure had inculcated in me those feelings, and thus to
respond with the appropriate sentiment. It was, in essence, an act of
dissimulation – but one which was necessary and appropriate. I'm
only informing you of the truth, as it were, because I have myself only
come to acknowledge it this morning. You did help me sleep, but
presently I'm no longer convinced of the need to sleep. Attached is a
rough calculation of the rent which you owe me for the last 6 months.
Perhaps if you 'sell' one of your paintings, you can find a way to pay
me back. I don't really need the money.

Liebe Grusse,

M________

"No Feeling…that's the issue here. Excellent, excellent – don't get me wrong…vast improvement from the previous draft…but where is the feeling?"

"Feeling?"

"Feeling…Market Feeling. Jesus how long have you been an analyst?"

"Five years."

"What other type of feeling is there?"

"None, I suppose, theoretically…but given the context, it seems inappropriate."

"How so?"

"Well…"

"Listen…I don't know how many times to drum this into your head…this is a great opportunity for you. But you're aware of this already…you need to trust my instincts here, I've seen different types of market in my time and many different iterations and versions…I've seen them rise, fall, stagnate, stutter, splutter, collapse, implode and explode. But there were feelings that preceded all of those events, and each had its own distinct one – feeling is the best and only indicator. This is no different. How can it be?"

7pm. An incidental durational experiment…the revisiting of a video for a song which, despite one's established tastes and predilections (at least those which are public) seems to be a triennial recurrence: 2009, 2012, 2015, 2019 *und so Weiter.* 'Listening in 2009! ☺', 'Watching this video for the 100th time today', 'Kill (((them))) all!', 'fixated with Thanatos…a runaway sub-program of Eros.' Charlotte, 24, Hackney Wick 'Hi, how are you this morgen?' 'I'm glad to detect in you a degree of self-interest…*Entschuldigung.*' 'I don't understand?' 'It's perfectly simple…mitigation strategies at this point are futile, and henceforth all strategies envisioned to attain maximum transactional velocity will no doubt also prove futile…only indicator = market feeling.' 'And how are *you* feeling today? How is your mental health?' 'My what?'

"Well, well, well…how are you mate? Least someone got their end away last night. Intern's looking for you…Here he is Ella, your boyfriend."

"Fuck off?"

"Course I will"

"How are you?"

"What's the feeling?"

"What? Listen…I guess it was a bit random last night, but I thought – yeah, we could like exchange numbers? And maybe go for dinner or something not at stupid o'clock?"

"…"

"Ok…I'll just leave it here."

"What's the feeling?"

"What does that mean?"

"The feeling."

"I feel like…I dunno…like we'd get on, maybe?"

"Sorry…yes, it's…the feeling is irrelevant. It doesn't exist. It's a myth."

"Oh…right, well, I'll take this back…and erm…bye, I guess."

She left. Midnight. Midnight. 11 hours. Note: Mitigation strategies should primarily concern themselves with bears, which tend to hide in the woods. What's the feeling? They feel nothing (insensitive). There was one particular bear, Urs was his name, who had a certain ursine joviality that instantly endeared people to him (her?). What a bastard! He knows what he's doing. Leading the poor market astray, with his ursine joviality and shit. Mitigation strategies. Blue Oceans. Gaussian. The regulatory authorities are primarily concerned with nature, which as we noted previously, is advancing in wrath. Important to bear (!) in mind.' 4am. I must sleep. I best sleep. Best sleep. I must be fresh. I lay (laid?) myself down to rest. *For a moment, my mind became clear. It was in the time of the fall. All things hushed to…sleep? No use in plagiarism at this point. Tomorrow will be a formative moment, as it always has been, and forever will be, until there are no more tomorrows left. I am incessantly haunted by the beyond. Philosophy is ultimately unconcerned with human weakness and frivolity, there is within it no accurate depiction of misery and despair — its origins are suspect, and its practitioners always died a good death, but good only in the sense that they died flabby and complacent — and of the very few that didn't, they were not philosophers at all - but prophets. All prophets are mad. Human existence was to be endured, not explained. Those who attempted an explanation may have satisfied themselves and their bootlickers with some crumb of cheap truth as ephemeral as the span of a human breath. But they no doubt renounced it, if they even thought of it at all (indeed who thinks of such frivolities?) when they drew that good last breath of their good death. Nothing more than fodder for the Annals composed by some sentient in the beyond. No difference between questions and answers.*

Alarm. 7am. I emerge reborn, revitalized, and step into shower. The water descended forcefully onto the marble floor and pummelled the sides of the glass cabinet. The water grew cold. I reach out my hand, which begins to shake. My head convulses sharply and rapidly, back and forth, as if it belonged to a marionette controlled by a spiteful and sadistic puppeteer. My tongue descends deep into my throat, as my knees give way, and I succumb to the warm, wet, darkness.

WOTSNAP[11]
Gina Rodrigues

[1] Matt and Pollyanne shoot a video

at first i was like wotevs – my big bro had an iphone 6 and id used it a bit when he wasnt looking to play angry birds. i was the same with concealer and blusher and that a year ago. i thort mum needs them cos shes old and old women have to look young but i am young so

then there was this app that connects to fb where u list who from ur fb friends u wanna do it with and if they say u then u get a dm that u like both wanna do it so u shud do. like tindr i guess. i was like meh but like then i was lowkey lovin it even tho its kinda lame. well at school doing it was swapped for getting off and most people who got a dm never actually got off cos they were frigid or were set up as a joke cos they were fraped or sumthin. sept melissa like cos she wasnt frigid of doing stuff. she was like ive been blobbing for 3 years so now im good to go and then she just got off with the first boy that dmed her. me and melissa were bezzies since primary school and steph and trace came

---

11 This story is set in early 2016, when almost all of it was written. Some small changes were made in 2017 and the story was finished in time for submission to this volume in early 2020. The story's staggered development has yielded several anachronisms that I have decided not to correct and therefore hope that the reader can forgive.

later but cos they had iphone 6s and they were up for doing stuff like melissa was melissa and them were more like bezzies than melissa and me by year 10. and also they started to be like u cant go thru school anymore without at least an ifone 6 and i was like guess ur right

so i asked mum can i have an ifone 6 for like both xmas and next birthday but early and she was like we cant afford it as a fam. i was like its not fair that jack my big bro has an iphone and i dont but she was like he used his own money but he didnt cos its his student loan money and its not really his. when i told her she was like hell pay the loan back when hes got a job so i was like ill get a job parttime in maccy ds or nandos or sumthin to pay for the iphone. she still sed no but i started crying and talking about cutting and cyber bullies and all that to scare her and she changed her mind

once i got my iphone i used it mostly for youtube and fb, just like what i did before on the pc downstairs in the dining room. the most different thing was i wud take selfies all the time. i wanted to get good profile pics and its hard to do that. melissas profile pic was perfect cos it was sexy but not slutty and shes really good at makeup. it was like her in a rocking chair in her dads home library or wotevs only with her dressing gown on after a bath and her hair was wet and the back of the rocking chair faces the door. the pic was taken from in the doorway with a timer and melissa is looking back over her shoulder like someone has creeped up on her and she didnt notice til the last minute cos she was concentrating dead hard on reading a book. so she looked clever and that but also ready to get off with someone. well i wanted a pic that was sorta like hers, so i googled arty pics of girls. some were bad like obvs photoshopped but the best ones were like alternatives or emos with tats and short hair that sat in like wooden chairs with their muffs out a bit. of course i didnt get naked but the tats were totes amaze so i got my big sis nat who does art at college to a draw a fake one on my back near my shoulder that was kinda half lizard and half dragon and then i copied melissas pic but i used a wooden chair from downstairs in a bare room with lots of natural lite which was basically the conservatory but with all the furniture taken out when mum and dad were at tesco

i posted the best pic and everyone was like wtf u got a tat. i lied and said that i went to watch my big bro get one and ended up getting one myself cos they thort in the shop i was his gf and over 18 too. i didnt feel bad cos i cudnt show my back at school sept in the changing rooms 4 p.e. and then i cud always wear a vesttop so noone wud see

btw the first thing i did when i got my iphone is download that app that tells u who wants to do it with who. well i chose all the boys that melissa said were hot and it said that 2 of them wanted to get off with me, matt and tom. at different dinnertimes at school i met them by the wall and we walked far enuff away from everyone and then we got off. i thort melissa was right that both boys were good at getting off and i liked it that it was kinda private even tho tbf his friends were watching us and my friends were watching us too

so anyways when i posted the tat pic matt and tom were like on facetime together at matts house and i started a chat and they were like show us ur tat and i did cos i hadnt washed it off yet and then they were laffing and saying stuff like show us ur tits too. i wasnt frigid or anything but i didnt want to cos i didnt want to look like a slut and too easy and also my tits werent that big compared 2 melissas at least. so instead i did a dance that was a bit sexy like on love island and showed my cleavage and they got out their six packs

a different time later i was dming just matt and he was like u can use this app to get around internet blocks and he also sent me a link too. when i clicked the link it was pornos but not like wot i thort with girls with fake tits and doing it in toilets instead it was hd quality with like insta filters and natural girls and hot boys that looked only a few years older than me. well i watched a lot of vids and i got swampy and everything. the girls looked like models from vogue and that and u cud tell that they were into it and not embarrassed or slutty cos they were so sexy and empowered and only empowered girls can properly control boys. even if they were just acting on camera i wud ship them so i rex they probably did it when the camera was off too. so the onscreen stuff was a bit like showing everyone how good u cud do it cos u did it offscreen too

another time matt dmed me and was like did u click that link and i said yes but i didnt like it cos it was disgusting and porn is only for boys. but he was like ur wrong and that bfs and gfs sometimes make their own pornos cos it makes them closer together. i googled it and found some forums and he was right. i knew what he was going to ask then and of course i wanted to but when he did ask i was like no. he was like we can practice a few times first. when we met up in town it was weird cos we didnt really talk at school cos he was always playing football and in different classes and wed only really done snapchat at night before that. i thort about asking trace or someone to come with me in case matt was a rapist or something but then i thort matt wud be upset and hes prob not a rapist so instead me and matt went nandos together then took the bus to his house. he showed me his drumkit and then we did it in his bedroom before his parents came back from work with a condom cos hed bought some from amazon. i cant even but it was like omg swipe right even tho matt was totes extra during the whole thing cos he thort he knew what he was doing and that. i was like we shud be secret bf and gf cos i didnt want everyone to say that im a slut and didnt want him to say i didnt actually have a tat and he said it was ok to keep it secret. he was gush at the time and he cudnt believe it and he didnt want me to leave even tho his parents wud cum home soon. so anyways i first lost my vs and then at other times we did things from the pornos like bjs and everything. i knew that perhaps i shud be more frigid but i was like wotevs cos i liked it and i knew that i cud tell melissa and steph and trace after theyd done more stuff than just getting off with peeps and getting fingered

i was always like mum im at stephs after school and she was like fine love have fun cos her and dad work late these days anyway. and after a while matt was my bae and it was funny cos at school we wudnt really speak or anything. when i got home from matts 1 time hed send snaps of his dick and i was like i saw this 2 hours ago u twat its nothing new and hed b a twat and say itd grown since i left his house and say funny stuff like that

so then during 1 wetbreak melissa was vicious cos steve had dumped her and then to me she was like u keep copying my profile pics and i love u dont get me wrong but sometimes ur just fucking basic. then steph was like u dont even have a tat i saw in p.e. when ur vesttop was thin and theres nothing there. i was gonna say something about laser surgery but then trace was like melissa ure obvs jelly AF cos of matt. i sent trace a screenshot of matts dick once cos she sent 1 of toms dick to me and i said never show anyone but she showed it to melissa when melissa called me fucking basic. melissa was like that cud be anyones dick but she was quiet afterwards

so my dads friend mr garner from the logistics company changed jobs and he is new at school and hes young for a teacher and hes the new tutor for our group. in tutor group 1 time mr garner was going on about the internet and he was like uve got to protect yourself against sex pests. nick was like are u a sex pest sir? but melissa was like thats not funny nick u gimp thats not an accusation to throw around litely its a serious problem and she smiled at mr garner cos mr garners actually quite fit and she thinks mr garner likes her and always looks down her cleavage on mufti days and at hockey. then mr garner was talking about twitter and online abuse and trace was like we dont use twitter much we use snapchat mostly. then trace told him how snaps disappear but peeps take screenshots and keep them and sometimes post them on fb. mr garner didnt know about this so he was upset and started banging on about cyber bullying and the stuff we always hear about in assemblies all the time

mr garner was getting boring so melissa was like btw sir u shud be aware that its not uncommon at this school in year 9 and 10 and 11 for certain students to possess certain uncompromising images of other certain students. mr garner was like in this school really? and melissa was like oh yes indeed even in this tutor group and she was looking down the row at me. mr garner was like images of female students? and he looked worried and melissa was like yes and also male students too and melissa looked at me even harder. it was so obvs that she was looking at me and mr garner was like melissa and pollyanne u 2 shud stay behind after this class and everyone was like oooo and nick sed jelly much melissa? and melissa turned around and she was like fuck off nick u gimp and everyone was like oooo even louder and nick got out his iphone and pretended to type and he was like oh matt oh matt let me suck u matt! and mr garner was like alright calm down for heavens sake and stop acting like children

then after class mr garner got v serious and closed the door and he was like melissa wot u said in class was v sensible cos accusations about any form of sexual harassment or extortion shudnt be thrown around litely esp in school where such matters are taken v seriously and are always investigated and melissa was quiet but said yes sir. mr garner said so are u making an official accusation here today? and melissa was like no sir but she wasnt looking at mr garner at all. mr garner sed so why did u say those things during class? and melissa was like i dont know sir im sorry sir its just that theres lots of pressure on young peeps these days and i wanted to emphasise to other peeps in the tutor group esp to the females or any transgenders if we have any of them in our tutor group that we shud be careful about online sex pests and everything but i guess i did that in the wrong way. mr garner was like well ur concern is admirable but the other students misunderstood ur message. melissa said yes sir and then mr garner was like pollyanne do u have anything to add to this discussion? and i was like no sir

next week miss stoddard was like pollyanne uve been asked to visit the headteachers office immediately and i had to leave french class with everyone watching me and i thort wtf cos i hadnt gone to the headteachers office by myself before. mrs pollock was there and even mum was there too and mrs pollock looked anxious but mum just looked like totes pissed off. And i was like shitting it cos i didnt really know what i was in trouble for tho obvs i had some idea cos of what melissa did. mrs pollock was like mr garner spoke to matthew worthing on friday and matthew told him that u and him are engaged in a sexual relationship. mrs pollock asked me is this true? and i went totes red and looked at mum and she kinda nodded towards mrs pollock sorta saying to me with her eyes u should answer mrs pollock cos i already know what ur gonna say. i was like yes miss weve been seeing each other for about 2 months now. and mrs pollock was like pollyanne did u and matthew ever shoot vids of u 2 engaged in sexual acts? and i didnt know what to answer cos i didnt know if saying yes or no wud get me and matt in more trouble and i started crying even tho i didnt want to just cos i didnt know what wud happen to me and matt. and then mrs pollock was like mr garner was made aware on friday that matt is in possession of such a vid and that u are present in that vid and i still didnt say anything cos i was crying and i just wanted her to say what wud happen to me and matt. and then mrs pollock was like pollyanne the next question is v important and i need u to answer and i just nodded my head cos i was crying and she was like did u agree to be in this vid? was it made with ur consent? and i nodded again and said we only made 1 vid and im really sorry

mrs pollock said that i appeared to be remorseful and me and matt are also underage which cud be problematic but they were mostly disappointed that i hadnt listened to the warnings theyd given us in assemblies about this stuff and i was incredibly lucky that matt hadnt posted the vid online cos that cud lead to a dangerous situation and hundo p ruin my life. i was still crying and was like im sorry i wasnt more careful and i guess now everyone will say im a slut and i prob deserve it and mrs pollock sed no uve been v brave today but there is a lot for u and ur mum to discuss in private and u are therefore excused from school until 2moz

so i went to mums work and sat in the waiting room and saw loads of sick peeps come and make appointments to see the doctor with mum at the reception desk and in the car afterwards i said look im really really sorry mum and she was like ive never been more embarrassed in my whole life and i thank god that none of those peeps actually watched ur filthy fucking porno cos i have to see them at parents evening and pta meetings all the time. then she was like u cudve at least had the dignity to wait til ud finished school or were at least 16 and i said im almost 15 and a half and nearly 16 and natalie says u were 16 when u first had sex and she was like thats regrettably true but i didnt tell anyone and i certainly didnt fucking film it and i said well i didnt tell anyone either its not my fault matt told mr garner and she said u wont b seeing that horny little bastard again and i doubt mr garner will be coming to see ur dad anytime soon with all the embarrassment uve caused us

so i didnt sleep much cos i was crying and mum and dad were rowing about school and mr garner downstairs anyway. in the morning i was like mum im sick please dont make me go to school. i didnt want to go cos everyone wud know me and matt were doing it and theyd be like ur a basic bitch and a slut and u lied about getting a tat. but mum was so angry and she made me go and i was totes surprised cos noone at school said anything to me about the vid. but like matt wasnt at school and mr garner told me after register he wont be at school again. and peeps were like has matt been expelled? but the teachers wudnt say and some peeps were like matts been arrested cos he made pornos with melissa and matt and mr garner watched them together and matts friends were like ur wrong matt made pornos with pollyanne but most peeps didnt believe that cos melissas got a reputation and i dont so

i dmed matt like wtf is happening with u but he never answered and matts friends said he cant use the internet anymore and his mum has confiscated his iphone. obvs i was dying cos he was my bae and i was literally going crazy but i didnt dare go 2 his house or anything. i actually went nandos a few times in case he was there but he wasnt and i kept posting pics of him and me on fb and saying i was lost without him and peeps were like oh is matt dead now? rip matt lets set up a memorial page on fb for him but thats just sum twats messing around who dont really know matt at all

i didnt get depressed or anything so i got over it and i was like it was only 2 months anyway even tho it was really special and ill never forget him cos he was my very first. dad got his mate nige to change something on my iphone and on the pc downstairs and then the internet block was back so i cudnt reach those sites matt showed me and so i wud remember our vid and i was like i wish had a copy cos the quality was better than webcam cos it was done on iphone 6 and its a sexy vid for girls and boys cos theres no muff or dick but u can see my tits and matts got a hot bod too

[2] Pollyanne's mother leaves

theyd not done divorce or anything but mum was living with nan for a bit and she said to me on the phone that she wasnt coming home until shed had enuff time to reflect and make some difficult decisions. dad was like batshit cos mum banned him from driving to nans or ringing her without prior permission and i cudnt stand it cos he was pacing up and down and trying to work out what to do and he was like u shudnt worry cos shell cum back any day now and i was like is she really mad or just stressed out and he was like yes i think it cud be stress and i was like is it my fault? and he hugged me and he was like no no sweetie pls dont think that even for a second. he was like that business with u and matt is all resolved and me and ur mum love u v much and cos he never said things like that and i usually hated hugging him i started to cry and say sorry again. of course i hadnt cried often at home since i was little not even to twilight cos its actually a pointless film and only in front of mum and never dad so it was all weird and v emotional

i mean dad thort i was like an actual child and i didnt have a clue but i was actually 1 of the best in my class in science even tho im in the bottom group and mr barstow sed theres no such thing as coincidence in science so i was like thinking mum leaving was totes my fault in fairness. so to help i googled stress and anxiety and divorce cos dads ok with old computer stuff like windows vistas and viruses but hes shit at google. i read about benzodiazepines and barbiturates but they can make u tranquilised like a horse or wotevs. and then when i cudnt find anything useful i was like maybe im stressed too cos im totes tired and i slept loads without thinking of mum or of anything at all. and i was like in my room most nights anyway before that but on fb or wotevs but then i was like i cant even be fucked with fb so i just lay on my bed and did a spotify sesh or took baths. 1 time mr garner came over to see dad and i was in my room on youtube and they were super quiet for like 3 hours but after that they were shouting and singing football songs til 3 oclock or something and i thort well its great that mr garner can help u take ur mind off this stuff with mum cos u need a break but will u just stfu please im trying to sleep

deep down was i was obvs guilty like im keeping mum away but on the surface i was like denying it to myself and i was thinking oh ill read this wiki about topping urself just cos im curious why these peeps do it but im above this stuff cos its like totes drama. and from the wiki it seemed more for boys than for girls anyway cos u see ur mate do it and then u get wrecked up and then u kill urself and its macho cos its a powerful message to other peeps and that. noone at my school was doing suicide anyway and i thort mum will probably come home soon cos noone can stomach nan for that long so just b patient and positive. tbh i was on spotify and on youtube more than thinking about cutting and topping myself and that stuff

so the whole time i cba with homework and hockey and tbh after two weeks i was like is mum back oh shes still away so the same as yesterday ok mayb shell come back 2moz then. mum being away and me doing fuck all was normal and dad didnt care about me doing nothing 1 bit. then i was like i need some action in my life. i thort mayb id do some cleavage snaps for random boys at school so i cud swap them for dick pics and build up my dick pic collection but that was over in like 2015 already and my cleavage isnt that big so. then i thort maybe id do solo cams for lolz and cos its pretty hot but then i was like id prob get tributes from paedos and thats it and besides theres the internet block. so instead i did loads of nude selfies so ive got loads of nude selfies to send to my next bf even tho i dont know who he is yet. i like hung my full length from the ceiling from the curtain pole thing to the lampshade so it was facing downwards and then took loads of pics where im like tangled up in the duvet and looking up helpless and i was like actually helpless cos the mirror is fucking heavy and it cudve fallen on me and killed me. and i did loads of selfies in the bath with bubbles and without bubbles and the bath is also good cos i cud like play with the water level and take underwater pics to a depth of 10 metres with this special iphone cover i got from amazon. i was like omg i can make my tits look bigger underwater this is great

tbh even doing selfies got boring cos i was like ive got no bf to send these selfies to. so in the end i was acting like a twat and making stupid pics like painting my lips and nips with lipstick like a clown or faceswapping my tits for babys faces from google images which is just wrong. i also did an underwater 1 in the bath where i put swimming goggles on my nips so they cud see underwater and i was honestly like lol this is fucking funny

my bro jack was back cos he cud skip uni for personal reasons cos mums away and he was like im here to support dad and the fam but he was literally down pub every night with gaz and some others. gaz was always a gimp anyway but he was worse now cos he was at uni and he sed oh im gareth now and when he spoke he sounded like harry potter even tho he was actually from heanor. and nat had this goth bf called seb and he was ok cos he offered me fags even tho i dont smoke cos it ages ur skin prematurely. hed be at our house all the time and him and nat wud fuck here cos they knew that dad didnt care atm. i cud hear it and sometimes i was jelly cos i thort of matt but it didnt make me swampy or anything cos sebs a great guy but hes a bit of a minger and nat cud do better cos she looks like the girl from twilight but with shorter hair and the main guy from twilight is totes hot i cant deny 1 time dad and mr garner were watching football downstairs and leicester won and they were celebrating and on the beers as per. and nat was sitting with them but mostly on her iphone cos seb was cooking something in the kitchen and i was like in the corner on the downstairs pc pretending to print something for school. and then dad was outside smoking and nat and seb were eating in front of the tv and mr garner was a bit wrecked up and he was like so hows the metal scene around here seb? u in a band urself? and seb was like so ur asking me and i wonder if uve ever asked nat cos she can shred better than i ever will and thats just gender normative. and mr garner was like ok i apologise hows the metal scene around seb and nat? and seb was like were in a band together and i sing and nat plays guitar and were called Apnea. mr garner laffed and he was like so thats a description of ur singing? and seb was like no thats just our name thx. and then mr garner asked were u bullied at school for being different seb? but seb didnt answer cos he pretended that he didnt hear. but then after a while seb was like its different to what u think cos peeps are tolerant nowadays and mr garner was like i doubt that v much. and mr garner was like its nice that u think that but in my experience peeps have learned to refrain from saying what they think but they think it anyway. mr garner was like i was bit like u when i was ur age but i didnt have the conviction to show it on a tshirt or to grow my hair like urs and i then i went to uni and the moment was gone. seb was like so howd u think peeps see me then? and mr garner was like it goes 2 ways either they see u as a smart but wayward boy thatll code for google someday or they see u as stoner without 2 brain cells to rub together. and seb was kinda angry and trying to provoke mr garner and he said so how do u urself see me then? and mr garner didnt answer but he just drank his beer in way that said i know better then to say anythin. nat was just quiet and stroking sebs hair and seb was like ive got to go home straight after this but before i go i want to say that u can feel superior if u like cos ur older than me but it doesnt count for anything and im sure ure a good teacher at pollys school but it doesnt mean u can pass judgement on me or nat or anyone else and mr garner was like im not judging anyone here seb u shudnt be so quick to play the victim. seb was like thats what im talking about and then nat and seb went into the kitchen and talked for a bit and then seb went home

so dad was drunk and he went upstairs to try and ring mum and mr garner was speaking to nat in the living room and i was still there and he was like did mr barstow ever make sexual advances towards u when u were at school? and nat was like no never. and mr garner was like that surprises me cos there are rumours that hes a bit hands on. nat was like so what surprises u is that the rumours are false or that he never tried anything with me? and mr garner was like clearly the latter cos i know the rumours are true. and nat was like so why does that surprise u? mr garner was like mr barstow has a type and that type is intelligent and sexually active young women and nat was like dyou think i fit this category? and mr garner was like well i wasnt ur teacher but i know this is true now. and then nat was like whats ur type? and mr garner was like when i met my wife she was also an intelligent and sexually active young women and nat was like im sure shes still intelligent and sexually active but is she still a young woman in ur eyes? and mr garner didnt answer

when nat went upstairs i followed her and i was like in her room and was getting ready for bed with her. and when nat was looking in her mirror at her own arse and i was sitting on her bed i said doesn't mr garner fancy his wife anymore? and nat was like why dyou ask are u volunteering to pityfuck him now matts out the pic? and i said well melissas always saying i shud leave my bedroom door open when im in bed when he comes over in case he gets curious about me and adventurous when he comes upstairs for the loo. and nat was like well melissa wud say that and you dont need to be curious to know that shes gonna grow up to be a bonerfidey fucking slag. i said well in that case shes only a wannabe slag cos she aint even lost her vs and besides mr garners too respectable to sleep with a virgin and nat was like laughing so hard and she was like i really dont think hed mind about that polly! and i sed well i mean he wont sleep with her cos she still in school anyway and thats why hes chatting up older women like he was chatting up u downstairs just now and nat was like im not an older woman and he wasnt chatting me up he was trying to beat his chest after a few beers and thats nothing new and tbh id feel sorry for him if i gave the tiniest shit about him at all. and nat was then on the bed with me and was stroking my hair in the same way she was stroking sebs hair earlier and she told me that men and boys think about girls all the time and they know that girls dont think about them cos girls have got better bodies and better things to do and boys are always trying to remind girls that theyre thinking of them. and she said that shes glad mums gone away cos shes taking a nice long break from dad and then she said that she sometimes felt like she wanted to fuck her girlfriends or fuck a clone of herself but she knows she ultimately needs a dick and sebs the best compromise cos he doesnt watch his own dick going in and out like most boys do. and i told her that i want mum to come home asap and that the best part of my vid with matt is defo my tits and that the vid wudve been even better if id had like a shoulder tat for real and melissa wud look shit with a shoulder tat cos shed look as cheap AF

[3] Pollyanne goes over to Melissa's

so school was just a mission at this point. i wasnt the best in my group at science anymore cos i cudnt be fucked with it and me and melissa werent bezzies anymore cos of matt. and trace and steph were being dickheads too cos they were like melissas must be a witch or something cos she made ur mum leave u cos she was jelly of u and matt and they wud laugh with each other but i just cudnt be bothered with that stuff cos its immature and not even funny and im not even into twilight or slender man or anything but then i was watching goblet of fire again 1 nite on the downstairs tv when nat was at sebs and jack was pubbing it but i was only watching it cos cedric diggory is the guy from twilight and hes obvs banging hot esp when hes like 18 in that film and in the film theyre talking about the repello spell that was put on the golden snitch. well melissa was like proper bumming harry potter at primary school and she went to the harry potter museum once in london or wotevs and i was like thinking obvs trace and steph are just being dickheads and not even funny but maybe theyre actually right about melissa being a witch and she did put a spell on mum after all. i didnt know how melissa got close enuff to mum to cast the spell but there is defo a motif cos melissa is still jelly of me and matt and her own mum is always proper wrecked up at bbqs and melissas always totes embarrassed about it so she might be jelly of my mum too

well anyways i was thinking like this for ages about how melissa cud get close enuff to cast the spell but i was also thinking like im going proper mental cos melissas a bitch these days and were not bezzies anymore but shed never hurt mum cos shes not really that bitchy and besides she didnt no how to cast a spell or poison anyone or wotevs cos shes like the worst in our group at science and we dont even do latin at our school. but still i was like obsessed with it even tho its immature. and anyway i was thinking about this stuff in the bath 1 time when melissa dmed me and she was like u shud cum over 2nite cos my bro is doing an xbox sesh with his mates and some of them are fit. first i was like wtf she wants to incantate me too cos ive worked out whats shes done but then i was like i shudnt be so fucking mental she prob just wants to get off with sum boys as per and she wants to do other stuff with them and shes finally got over herself and wants some tips on bjs and bum beads and that cos shes prob actually frigid and ive done that stuff with matt like a hundo times

so she was like come thru the backdoor and straight up to my room cos weve gotta put on some slap before going to watch the guys play xbox. she wasnt bitchy and we were like bezzies again and i was like thinking oh maybe she did the repello spell on mum bcos its kind to make mum stay away so she can have a break from dad but then i was like know melissas just being nice to me cos steph and trace arent here and otherwise shed still be bitchy

i was lucky cos i was already wearing my skinny jeans with holes in the knees and melissa put her skinny jeans 2 and we did the blusher in natural tones cos its important not to overdo it and we watched a youtube vid for how to achieve the smoky eyes effect. and melissa was like i cba with guys from school now esp matt cos theyre immature and they cant handle real women who are assertive like u and me. she was like we shud focus on older guys and leave the boys at school to steph and trace cos steph and trace need every chance they can get cos theyre fucking hopeless and besides theyve been bad examples of feminism recently

so when we went downstairs to the living room melissas bro was there with like 4 or 5 mates and they were xboxing and melissas bro was like fuck off melissa were xboxing in here tonight and its a boys nite and melissa was like its my house too and anyway me and polly are just coming in to say hi and to be civilised cos weve got our own girls nite planned later. melissas bro was like well actually its mum and dads house not urs but he wasnt really bothered cos he was xboxing and his mates didnt say anything and they were totes silent and they werent even looking at us properly so melissa just sat in an armchair and i sat on the arm of the chair. i mean it was totes awkward to start with cos me and melissa were watching them playing fifa but everyone knew we didnt care about fifa 1 bit and noone wud speak to us. but then 1 of melissas bros friends asked me to play fifa with him and i was shit but it broke the ice and then most of them wud speak to us a bit and esp keiran who is like in year 11 and was even fucking chloe hargreaves for a bit and shes easily the hottest girl in school so

melissas bro went all mardy but the other guys got flirty pretty quickly like keiran put his hands over my eyes when i was playing so id lose the game. it was like proper romcom cheesy but by this time id totes forgot about checking melissas wardrobe for acult symbols and all that immature stuff and tbh i was thinking about some of the good pics id taken with the full length hanging from the ceiling and perhaps id send them to keiran but only if he sent me something first

melissas bro was having a proper mard and hed fucked off sumwhere and so melissa was getting off with this guy alex who was defo v attractive and in year 11. and me and keiran were going to get off and i cud tell cos he kept getting closer to me and wed been snapping in secret for an hour or so. the other guys were pretending not to see anything and i wudnt have cared anyway cos it was okay before when peeps watched at school. and then this guy who looked proper fucked on xan and almost passed out and who had been sitting in the corner the whole time and had said nothing all night took his headphones off and was like staring at me and then he was like hold on do i know u? i was like maybe cos ive been on the year 11 hockey team a few times and he was just staring at me like a totes spazmoid and was like no i know u from somewhere else have u got a vlog or something? i was like err no and then he started laffing and shaking his finger at me and he said ah i think u just remind me of a girl i saw in vid once and it was a fucking great vid if you know what i mean! and he was still laffing and shaking his finger and by this point melissa and alex had stopped getting off and i was so embarrassed i cudnt bring myself to look at this crazy guy or at anyone else in the room or even at the paused fifa game on the tv and so i just looked at melissa and she knew that i wanted her to say something but she just stayed super quiet and in fact nobody said anything at all. finally keiran was like tim ure barred out bruv u dont know what ure on about and then melissas bro appeared in the room from nowhere with a beer in his hand and he was like well thats a roundabout way of saying that u wanna pop pretty pollys cherry isnt it timmy boy? well why dont u 2 stop beating around the bush and get to it and stop ruining our fucking xbox sesh. and this barred out guy got confused and he was like no no bruv i just saw this vid with a girl that looked like her and thats all im saying. i swear i was dying at this point cos my cheeks had flushed so much and i cudnt move my neck to look up and see them all sitting there and i felt panicked cos i thort i cud see melissa from the corner of my eye with her iphone out filming everything. then melissas bro put on this fake apologetic voice and was like oh no sorry ive got that wrong u cant pop pretty pollys cherry cos shes already fucking matt wortho and they made a porno and thats prob where uve seen polly before and the weird guy was like but i thort melissa was fuckin matt wortho?

i just got up and left the house without looking up at anyone. i wanted to cry but i cudnt cos i was still embarrassed and not upset. it was dark and i was cold cos id forgotten my coat and when melissa caught up with me she was wearing her own coat but she hadnt bought mine. she was like polly u shuda seen alexs face lite up when tim said about me and matt cos now he knows im up for it and so i reckon if i go back and rip a crotch hole in some tights and wait in my room til like 2am or something then alexll make an excuse to stay over and my bro will be asleep and alexll slip into my room and then hell eat me out. i didnt feel embarrassed anymore just angry at melissa for being such a dumb bitch and at myself for forgetting that she was such a bitch and so i was like ure fucking mental we both know uve never even been with matt or with any boy so why are u pretending like u know anything about sex other than flickin ure bean and taking way 2 many selfies of ure own fat tits? and then i ran home as fast as i cud before she cud say anything or catch me at all

when i got home mr garner was sitting on the sofa watching tv with 1 eye shut cos he was obvs hundo p slammed. he just smiled at me like drunk peeps do and he didnt even notice i was out of breath from running. i was like err so wheres dad and he was like oh pollyanne i need to ring my wife can you pass me my phone please its somewhere on the sideboard. i looked and i cudnt see it but tbh i didnt look too hard cos i was desperate for the loo. i was like i cant see it and he sed its there sumwhere and i was like just use mine i regretted not having my iphone in the loo cos i wanted to see wot melissa had dmed me. i rexd shed either be like are u gonna say sorry now or wot or shed pretend i didnt say anything and tell me how she was waiting for alex in her slaggy tights. i kinda felt sorry for her cos i knew she actually wud wait in bed all nite for no reason but i didnt feel sorry for v long cos she obvs doesnt care about anyone but herself and also cos i knew shed be lying about how she fucked alex at school for months after this and it wud totes do my head in

mr garner musta been like hypnotised by the tv or something so i just took my iphone off his knee without saying anything and sat down next 2 him and he didnt even move 1 bit. i had 2 notis and i thort they were from melissa but they were from keiran. the first sed he was thinkin of me and the second was a pic of his dick. i was about to start scrolling thru my gallery for a sexy bath pic when i saw that somehow id started a convo with someone called john garner and when i clicked into the convo i saw that id shared loads of my nude selfies with him

i cant describe it but this like panic and shock came over me and made me feel heavy and stupid and slow and without meaning to i looked up and across at mr garner and all of sudden he was sitting upright and staring at me. he cleared his throat and said:

i'm going to show them to matt, that's all. i swear it: that's all i'm gonna to do. i hardly saw anything myself, and i don't want to! matt and i are good friends, we've been friends for a while now and i know how much he misses you and i thought that these photos would definitely cheer him up and keep the fires of romance burning between you two while you're apart and he's not allowed to see you. i mean, they're meant for him anyway, right? i know its wrong for me to just send them to myself without asking you first, but i saw them on your phone and i thought of matt and i just sent them impulsively. please don't be upset, polly, please! i promise you that i won't look at them, and that i won't show them to anyone but matt. you'd like him to see them, right? he really misses you. i'm honestly just the messenger here. i mean if you think about it, its pretty obvious that i'm doing matt a huge favour here and putting myself on the line. i'm a married man, i'm your teacher, and i'm your dad's pal. so please let me be a good friend to him – and to you – and trust me to be discreet. and i'm banking on you keeping this quiet, so that it'll be a complete surprise for matt. and also so everything goes smoothly. i mean, if your mum or dad finds out, they'll kick up a fuss and matt'll be in trouble all over again. he'll probably be banned from seeing you or from using a smartphone for his entire life. and we need … look, it's a lot to take in, right? i've clearly dropped a huge bombshell here. i guess i should've told you about my friendship with matt before. i'm sorry about that. but i didn't want to give you false hope. keeping you in the dark was my way of protecting you. you're okay, right? right? that's it, that's it, good … good. things will okay between us, i think. right?